THE WOMAN ON THE ROOF

By Helen Nielsen

Black Gat Books • Eureka California

THE WOMAN ON THE ROOF

Published by Black Gat Books
A division of Stark House Press
1315 H Street
Eureka, CA 95501, USA
griffinskye3@sbcglobal.net
www.starkhousepress.com

ISBN: 978-1-944520-13-7

Book design by Mark Shepard, SHEPGRAPHICS.COM

First Black Gat Edition: November 2016

First Edition

"Singularly satisfying."
—Anthony Boucher, *New York Times*

"Best whodunit of the year."
—*Springfield News and Leader*

"Among the best mysteries of the year."
—Mystery Writers of America

"With its crisp descriptions of setting
and amusing metaphors, this book deserves a high rank among California's
many whodunits."
—Don Napoli, *Reading California Fiction*

"Why not start by acquainting yourself
with Helen Nielsen's work? You're
sure to come back for more."
—John F. Norris, *Pretty Sinister Books*

HELEN NIELSEN BIBLIOGRAPHY
(1918-2002)

SIMON DRAKE SERIES

Gold Coast Nocturne (1951; reprinted in pb as Dead on the Level, 1954; UK as Murder by Proxy, 1952)

After Midnight (1966)

A Killer in the Street (1967)

The Darkest Hour (1969)

The Severed Key (1973)

The Brink of Murder (1976)

NOVELS

The Kind Man (1951)

Obit Delayed (1952)

Detour (1953; reprinted in pb as Detour to Death, 1955)

The Woman on the Roof (1954)

Stranger in the Dark (1955)

Borrow the Night (1956; reprinted in pb as Seven Days Before Dying, 1958)

The Crime is Murder (1956)

False Witness (1959)

The Fifth Caller (1959)

Sing Me a Murder (1960)

Woman Missing and Other Stories (1961)

Verdict Suspended (1964)

Shot on Location (1971)

CHAPTER ONE

A peculiar ritual took place every evening when Wilma Rathjen came home from work. It began with the snapping of the wall switch that turned on all of the living-room lamps, then the bolting of the door behind her, and then a careful tour of inspection throughout the three rooms and bath that comprised her garage apartment. Was the wing chair out of position? Were the shutter screens ajar? Had the magazines been moved on the cobbler's bench? Nothing was too insignificant for the attention of this small woman with a sprinkling of middle-age gray in her dark hair and a nameless fear in her searching eyes. Even the closets were examined to make sure each modest garment was still pinned securely inside its paper jacket and each shoe was free from the evidence of unauthorized wear. Only when the ritual was completed could she respond to the greeting of a huge yellow cat that rubbed eagerly against her spindly legs, while throbbing a hymn of praise for the package of pork liver in her shopping bag.

... But one night the ritual was omitted.

It was Waggoner's fault. Not that the day hadn't been difficult before she came on duty, but Leota Waggoner, the manager of store 217, Old Country Style Bakeries, Inc., had the eyes of a hawk and the soul of a gauleiter. Wilma had no more than entered the shop when the torment began.

"What about your birthday cake, Miss Rathjen? Has your customer come for it yet?"

The question was superfluous. A four-layer cake with chocolate icing, pink sugar roses, and *Happy Birthday Darling* scrawled across the top was certainly obvious among the regular stock. So was Waggoner's interest.

"I do hope you haven't made another mistake," she added ominously. "I don't know what the supervisor's going to say if you have!"

That was the beginning of it. One suggestion from Waggoner and Wilma's troubles multiplied. Birthday cakes were special order, and strange things were always happening to the special orders she wrote up—like the six cakes for the P.T.A. that came in a week early and the ninety dozen doughnuts for the church social that never came in at all! It wasn't that Wilma was stupid—she'd been head of her class at teacher's college until she had to quit—but with so many terrible things going on in the world (some under her very eyes!), the dull details of a customer's wishes frequently found no lodging in her crowded mind. Yet there was no mistake about the birthday cake. She remembered that order only too well!

There were times when nature itself seemed to conspire against Wilma Rathjen. Rainy days made her nervous, and so it became a rainy day. The low fog (pronounced "drizzle" everywhere but in Los Angeles) reached the status of a deluge by midafternoon and had the older customers wistfully recalling the lovely winters before those fool scientists began playing with atom bombs. But any hope Wilma cherished that her sale could be written off to the weather was short-lived.

"A customer who can afford a five-ninety-five cake can afford a taxi," Waggoner decreed. "A little rain can't wash out a birthday!"

Perhaps not, Wilma conceded silently, but something else can.

Like all Old Country Style Bakeries, store 217 was located in a large market at a busy intersection. Ordinarily Wilma walked through the market on her way home—it was handier to the boulevard, and she liked the brief sense of belonging that came from nodding good night to fellow employees along the way—but on this particular evening she sneaked out the back way. The reason was obvious. In addition to the shopping bag, a handbag, and an umbrella, Wilma carried an enormously large cake box that had spent the better part of the afternoon hidden behind a trash can in the stockroom. She was going to miss that $5.95, but not nearly so much as she'd miss her job if Waggoner found the cake in the checkout. The job was much more than a pay check (Curtis would never let her starve)—it was an escape from sitting alone in her tiny apartment, listening, watching, until her mind began to play tricks again and she'd have to go back to that terrible place. The mere thought of it made her shudder. Thank God, Waggoner hadn't seen her leave!

The service door of the bakery opened out on a wide parking lot that separated the market from La Rene's Place, a neon-striped nitery noted for somewhat more than its cuisine. By this time the hills above Santa Monica Boulevard were wrapped up for the night in a dusky gray blanket of rain, but the floodlights were on at La Rene's, and the scantily clad ladies on the outdoor posters smiled vacantly at the storm. Wilma always walked at a fast, flatfooted gait that made it appear she was trying to catch up with someone just ahead, and she walked even faster past the smiling ladies. It seemed that their smiles were at her expense, and their seductive eyes held some evil spell. What right had the bad to be beautiful when Wilma Rathjen was so plain?

But she mustn't think such things. She hurried on, trying to recall the words of a favorite Psalm that would exorcise the faces from her mind, and then a voice called out above the drumming rain.

"Miss Rathjen! Is that you, Miss Rathjen? Hop in and I'll drive you home."

There was no reason to be afraid. The voice was familiar, and she recognized the small sedan, and yet Wilma shrank back.

"Don't worry about the upholstery," urged the young woman who leaned across the seat to hold open the door.

"A little rain can't hurt this crate."

Wilma wasn't worried about the upholstery. Wilma was worried about that oversized cake box and how she would explain it if Ann Jenner made an inquiry. She knew how much use Wilma Rathjen would have for a party cake!

"I really enjoy walking," she began, but Ann wouldn't hear of it.

"In this downpour! There's enough flu going around without you giving us trouble, too!"

The white uniform showing under Ann's raincoat would have explained that statement even if Wilma hadn't known that she was a nurse. And Wilma didn't like nurses. They were too brisk and efficient and worldly wise—she doubted that they were very moral. But Ann Jenner wasn't a hospital nurse; she was nurse-receptionist for Dr. Fergus, whose office was in the medical center just around the corner from the market, and she lived in the north front unit of the same bungalow court. Because of these things, and the fact that she could think of no way out, Wilma climbed into the front seat alongside Ann and tried to camouflage the cake box with the shopping bag, the handbag, and the dripping umbrella.

"You're off early today," Ann remarked, steering back into the line of traffic.

"It's Wednesday," Wilma muttered.

"Oh, that's right. You open the store Wednesdays, don't you? How do you like your job by this time?"

Wilma didn't answer. She would just as soon not discuss anything pertaining to the bakery on this particular evening—as for being early, if it hadn't been for that unhappy coincidence, she wouldn't be fretting so about the cake box! But like all the nurses Wilma had known, this one had to go on chattering and prying.

"This is quite a coincidence," she said. "Doctor Fergus was inquiring about you only this afternoon."

Wilma tensed. "What did Doctor. Fergus want to

know?" she asked.

"Nothing in particular. He merely asked how you were getting along."

"Doctor Fergus is not my doctor!"

Wilma didn't catch the brief smile that did so much for the nurse's rather plain face. "I'm sure the doctor wasn't trying to drum up trade," she remarked. "It was seeing your brother's picture in the paper that made him think of you. Have you seen it, Miss Rathjen?"

The local sensation sheet was still folded tightly inside Wilma's shopping bag, but she didn't have to see the picture. The pictures of Curtis were always the same—his pudgy face smiling from the head of some banquet table and a gavel clutched firmly in one hand. Pictures were about all she saw of Curtis any more. She sometimes wondered if that gavel was a part of him now.

"He's getting to be a big man in this town," Ann added, and Wilma began to feel a little ill. A big man. They were the very words Curtis had used the day he drove her from the sanitarium to her new home. Some people couldn't understand why Curtis Rathjen's sister lived in the most unpretentious of his rentals, but the tiny apartment above the garage had been built especially for her. There she could have privacy. No voices on the other side of a thin partition, no windows at ground level, no unexpected footsteps in the hall.

"You won't be bothered by the neighbors up here," he promised her. "There's just one stairway, and no one to use it but you. But watch yourself. Any more tall tales to the police and you're going back to that sanitarium to stay! I can't afford any more bad publicity. I'm getting to be a big man in this town."

They were words Wilma would never forget. Suddenly she began to tingle with excitement. Was it really just a coincidence that Ann Jenner had picked her up on her one early day? Was it a coincidence that she used Curtis's exact words? And Dr. Fergus had inquired about her. From some pale memory came the knowledge that Curtis once mentioned meeting this Dr. Fergus at his club. Could it have been more than a casual meeting? Was the neighborhood doctor supposed to make inquiries and the north front tenant supposed to watch?

"Aren't you feeling well, Miss Rathjen?"

Wilma looked up and saw how the nurse was staring at her haggard reflection in the driving mirror. "I'm just tired," she said quickly. "I had a difficult day."

"Just the same, I think I'll see you upstairs and take your temperature. You don't want to take chances in weather like this."

No, I don't, Wilma thought. *I don't want to take chances in any kind of weather—not with a clever one like you!* Nurses could be as bad as doctors—or even policemen. They listened, and were sympathetic, and even encouraged you to tell all the terrible things you knew; but all the time they were making plans to put you away— It was only six blocks from the market to the bungalow court, and Wilma had her door open before the sedan stopped rolling.

"I wouldn't think of troubling you," she cried before the nurse could make any protest. "I'll just have a light supper and get right to bed. No, don't help me! I can manage!"

It wasn't very wise to shout so much, but she couldn't have the woman pawing at the cake box. Wouldn't that make a nice report to take back to Curtis? Your sister is sick again. She bought herself a big birthday cake, and it isn't even her birthday! Scooping up everything together, and without so much as a "Thank you for the ride," Wilma turned and fled down the narrow center walk that led to the garage stairs. She didn't stop running until she was upstairs and locked safely inside her own small sanctuary.

How long she stood there staring at the cake box in her hand Wilma never knew. She had forgotten the light switch. The room came gradually into focus as a study of shadows made by the streaming dusk and the lights from the court below. She was wet and chilled through, and the dripping umbrella was making an unsightly pool on her braided chenille rug, but still she stared at the cake box. Now it seemed to be the evidence of the most foolish thing she had ever done.

"Any more tall tales to the police," Curtis warned out of the gloom, "and you're going back to that sanitarium to stay!"

But how was she to know? How could she distinguish the tall from the true? It was trouble at the bakery if no customer came to pay for the cake—but what if the customer did come?

Wilma had to know. There were six units (not including the garage apartment) in the court—three each in two rectangular buildings that were joined in the front by a stucco arch. Three identical doors faced three identical mates, and each ribbon of light that fell across the narrow patch of center green marked the living-room windows of a separate unit. Ann Jenner's light was showing when Wilma stepped to her own front windows and peered out. The opposite number was dark; a handsome young man like Tony Carmen seldom kept his long convertible at home. The ribbon of light behind Ann Jenner's meant that old Wallace Timm was at home, as usual, and across from his apartment the lights always blazed and the radio blared. This was the den of what Wilma called "the theatricals," and she did wish that Curtis would learn not to rent his apartments to giddy young girls from the near-by little theater.

But there were six units in the court, and it was the last two that gave Wilma so much trouble. From her high vantage point she could see much more of these apartments than mere ribbons of light. She could look down into the windows of two kitchens, two bedrooms, and two baths; and it was appalling how few people ever thought to lower the blinds. Not Ruby Lennox, surely. Ruby had no more secrets than a confession magazine. But it wasn't the view of Ruby's apartment that Wilma strained to see.

Her eyes traveled across the court. The bathroom window was bright again—at least that much wasn't just in her mind. Her heart began to beat faster. Moments ago a thought had come like late sunshine. Even if she had made another mistake, there was a way out. She could deliver the cake herself and say it was just a special service because of the storm. Beautiful girls accepted service as a natural right, and Jeri Lynn was the most beautiful girl Wilma had ever seen.

But the bathroom window was still bright and everything inside just as she'd remembered it all day: the head thrown back, the auburn hair floating on the water, the naked shoulders showing brown against the stark white of the tub.

Wilma stepped back from the window with a sigh of relief. She'd been right, after all. Jeri Lynn wouldn't call for her birthday cake.

CHAPTER TWO

Because Ruby Lennox couldn't pay her telephone bill, the body in the bathtub was discovered the next morning. It was almost noon, but Ruby was still wearing just a coolie coat and slippers when the telephone serviceman pounded on her door.

"You might at least give me time to finish breakfast," she muttered over the coffee cup in her hand. "Some people work nights, you know."

The telephone man grinned over his private opinion of

this tousled blonde's night work and went inside the apartment, but Ruby stepped out on the tiny cement porch to drink in a little sunshine with her coffee. It felt good after all the rain, and it always surprised Ruby to wake up and find a world so clean and fresh and free of cigarette smoke, stale liquor odors, and a background music of banging trays. Ruby was a waitress by trade, on a six-to-two shift, but she seldom got to work before seven or came home before dawn. Home, she had learned, could be the loneliest place in town.

But there was nothing lonely about the courtyard this bright and shining morning. The storm had passed in the night, and now an old man in baggy overalls and a faded blue shirt was out raking up dead leaves and palm fronds from the narrow parkway that separated the two buildings. The sight of any living creature was a signal for Ruby to strike up a conversation.

"You're working too hard, Pop," she called out, and the old man turned around and frowned at her with his withered-apple face.

"Rathjen don't think so," he muttered. "Rathjen don't think I do any work at all."

"Yeah? And what does Rathjen do besides collect the rent?"

The old man—that's how Ruby always thought of him although he might have been anywhere from fifty to seventy—seemed to think the question worthy of consideration. He leaned on the rake and gazed at the open door beyond Ruby's shoulder. All that activity inside had to mean something. People usually had the phone taken out when they were going to move, and if Ruby was moving, Rathjen would want to know about it right away. Curtis Rathjen didn't like his rentals standing vacant.

"Anything wrong?" he asked, and Ruby, who would recite every incident of her colorful life on less of an opening than that, launched into a sad story of what can happen to a phone bill if a lady gets a load on and starts calling long-distance everybody she's ever known.

"It's a helluva note," she reflected sadly. "I get lonesome as it is. Without a phone how does a gal make any dates?"

"I've got a few dollars—" the old man began.

"Thanks, Pop, but this bill happens to be for thirty-eight bucks. Who's got money like that?"

It was a sobering thought, and both the old man and Ruby observed an appropriate silence. Then Ruby tossed her silver-blond head and grinned because life was too full of ups and downs to get low over anything so trivial as having a phone jerked out.

"Maybe Rathjen's got a few chores I could do," she said, "—or has that job been taken?"

Ruby looked directly across the courtyard as she spoke, and a certain edge on her words seemed to embarrass the old man out of further conversation. Muttering something about a leaky rain gutter, he dropped the rake and ambled off toward the garage. When he returned a few minutes later with a ladder under his arm, the serviceman was all finished with Ruby's phone, and the two of them were chatting on the porch like a pair of old friends. But the sight of the ladder spoiled that.

"Hey, Pop," the man called out, "how's about borrowing that? I've got to check this line, and it'll save me a trip to the truck." So the serviceman took the ladder around to the rear of the south unit where the wires came in, and a few minutes later he came galloping back with his eyes bulging and his mouth wide open.

"There's a dead woman in the bathtub!" he yelled. "Lemme use a phone!"

She was dead all right, good and dead. The eager lad who had called for the Pulmotor was a couple of days late, and it didn't take a coroner's report to convey that knowledge to an old hand like John Peter Osgood. Osgood had seen plenty of corpses in his forty-odd years, and the only thing unusual about Jeri Lynn's was that a beautiful girl found dead in a shabby rear apartment usually didn't die so clean. It was a little disappointing. Murder, now, was something a man could get interested in. The blindfolded lady usually had the edge in the death-by-violence department, and the blindfolded lady was a kind of personal ward of Osgood's. She took the place of other loves he'd never had.

"It's like they always say," Frenchy observed. "More people get killed in bathrooms than any place else. That's why I stay dirty."

Frenchy Bartel wasn't at all dirty. He was as elegant in his checked sport coat and flannel slacks as Osgood was drab, but then, Frenchy didn't look like a policeman. He could pass for a procurer, a young hood, or an H pusher— and had on other details; but there was something about John Peter Osgood's solid body and blunt-featured face that seemed to make the badge show right through the pocket of his dark-gray worsted. Maybe that was because Osgood had inherited his job. A likeness of his father in full uniform still occupied the same place on the mantel as it had the day a trigger-happy hoodlum had made Mrs. Osgood, Senior, a widow, and Osgood Junior had subsequently racked up nineteen years of retirement time trying to even a score everybody else had forgotten. He'd finally made a sergeant's rating and really didn't expect to do much better. With his pay and Ma's pension there was no great need. He didn't have to buy mink coats and imported perfume for any lovely extravagance like the dead girl in the tub.

The story appeared simple enough. The tub was an old-fashioned model with the side plastered up to make it look built in, and where the narrow end fitted into the corner the plaster formed an edge about ten inches wide. Above the ledge was an electric outlet with an appliance cord still plugged in, and at the bottom of the tub was a hair dryer that didn't mix well with water. The room smelled of colognes and the varied ingredients of a lady's beauty magic; a filmy dressing gown was draped over the hamper, and in the adjoining bedroom a full-skirted dinner gown was spread out in readiness on the bed. A lady with a heavy date, the evidence said, could get awfully careless with her timesavers.

"Honey, why did you have to wash your hair?" Frenchy moaned, and then stepped aside for the boys from the meat wagon.

Osgood never had much to say. Be it homicide, suicide, or just plain stupidity, there was still the bookwork to be done. His eyes recorded the same details that Frenchy saw, and maybe a bit more, but through it all his mind was busy on the report. Name: Jeri Lynn (this from the excited tenants outside)—female—white—age 20-22— next of kin—

"Next of kin," he said aloud. "I wonder if anybody knows who that might be."

By this time half of the neighborhood had gathered in that long courtyard, and it was a little difficult to cull out the residents from the curiosity seekers. But Frenchy finally came up with an old man who said his name was Wallace Timm and that he was a caretaker of sorts.

"All I know is that she lived here alone," he said. "She had callers sometimes, but I don't think they were relatives."

"Men callers?" Frenchy asked.

The old man scratched his graying head with a hand that was minus a couple of fingers. "Mostly," he admitted, "but she was friends with the girls next door, too. They're in the same business."

"What business is that?" Osgood asked.

"Show business. I think she used to model some, too. And she told me one time that she was a starlet."

"Starlet," Frenchy murmured. "That's Hollywood for photogenic female, unemployed."

Frenchy was the expert on the subject of anything female, but Osgood frowned. The apartment was cheap enough, but the dress on the bed and that filmy item in the bathroom hadn't come out of unemployment checks.

"Where was she from?" he asked, and the old man shook his head.

"That I wouldn't know. Never talked to her much unless something needed fixing—like the other day when the bathroom lock was sticking and she had me take the bolt out so's it couldn't lock her inside."

"Apparently she didn't like locks. I understand all the doors were unlocked when you found her."

"That's right. She never locked up unless she was going away. Anyway, I remember seeing that hair dryer at the end of the tub when I was working on the door. I told her that was a dangerous place to keep it, but she didn't listen. Young people never think about danger."

"Or much of anything else," Osgood muttered. "All right, Frenchy, stop drooling and go after the girls next door."

Frenchy took the old man out with him, and by that time the apartment was empty except for Osgood. He went back into the bathroom for another look at that hair dryer. It was a simple hand type, but the handle folded down to form a stand. It didn't weigh much, but he ran his hand over the painted plaster ledge to pick up any indentation. After that, he put the dryer aside and went into the bedroom to have a look at the closets. As he expected, they were loaded with finery to match that gown on the bed and included a mink coat. It wasn't unusual for a beautiful girl to put every dime she made on her back, but mink did run into an awful lot of dimes.

All of the furnishings were bargain-center specialties. Next to the bed stood a small table that held a lamp, a telephone, and a book of personal phone numbers. Osgood opened the book and thumbed through it quickly. It seemed to be just a collection of first names (masculine) with a few business cards tucked in between the pages. A doctor, an actor's representative, a commercial photographer— The noon whistle sounded in the distance, and Osgood reacted with an automatic check of his wrist watch. It was beginning to look as if Jeri Lynn's next of kin might be a little difficult to locate, but his own next of kin would be waiting for that daily call. He pocketed the book of personal numbers and reached for the phone.

Osgood was still telephoning when Frenchy came back.

"... Sure, Ma, I've got it all written down: eggs, oranges, and stop at the drugstore for more of your nerve tonic. Now don't bother fixing dinner if you don't feel like it. I can pick up something on the way home."

The conversation ended abruptly when Osgood looked up and found three pair of eyes staring at him. He slammed the phone back in the cradle and ignored Frenchy's twisted grin. Frenchy seemed to think there was something wrong in a man calling his mother every noon for nineteen years.

"Well?" he snapped, and everybody got down to business.

The girls Frenchy had brought along were a couple of shapely kids who would never see eighteen again. One was a long-legged redhead named Sharl, and the other a diminutive brunette who called herself Denise. They were both co-operative and eager. "Poor Jeri! Darling Jeri! Of course, we knew her intimately!" But intimately in their jargon could mean something as casual as a three months' speaking acquaintance with no knowledge whatsoever of her origins or family.

"The trumpet player might know," Sharl suggested. "That's Tony Carmen up front. I think he used to date her some."

"Or Ann Jenner," Denise added. "She's up front, too—across the court. She's a nurse, and she's lived here even longer than Jeri."

Osgood passed a silent signal to Frenchy, and Frenchy sighed. "Just when I was enjoying the view," he muttered.

"Take the view with you," Osgood said. "No, wait a minute. Just when was the last time either of you girls saw your intimate friend alive?"

Two studied frowns worked over the question. Denise answered first.

"Tuesday afternoon. I was on my way to the theater for rehearsal and I saw her going into Elaine's—that's a beauty shop up on the boulevard. We rehearsed until practically curtain time and I never saw her again. Did you, Sharl?"

"No, but I heard the bath water running," the redhead said. "The plumbing in this run-down dump is terrible. Turn on a faucet in any apartment and the whole court rumbles."

"And what time was this?"

"Tuesday evening. It must have been around six-thirty or seven. Jeri always ran a bath before she went out to dinner, and she always had a dinner date— Golly, think of her lying in here dead all that time!"

Frenchy got the girls out before they had a chance to run through all of their dramatic lessons, but as far as bringing back any information, his trip was just a lot of exercise. The nurse worked until after five, the trumpet player doubled on an instrument known as a tote board, and when the track was fast, Tony Carmen was gone—that was the gist of the report Frenchy brought back from his travels. By that time Osgood had completed his tour of inspection through the apartment. He'd peeked into a kitchen with a few dirty dishes in the sink and a bottle of freshly opened Scotch out on the drainboard, tried the back door and found it unlocked as reported (a matter he quickly rectified), and finally returned to the small and dingy living-room. There was a spindly-legged desk that contained a stack of unpaid bills, a checkbook showing a bank balance of $3.60, and an assortment of glossy publicity photos that weren't much help since they were all of the dead girl. It didn't seem right. There should have been a few snapshots with faces he could fit names to, and a few personal letters with a return address in the corner.

"Does that account for everybody in the court?" he asked Frenchy.

"Well, there's an old girl living on the roof."

"On the what?"

"The garage roof. There's a new garage with an apartment built on top. But she's not at home, either. And then there's a blonde just across the way who reminds me of something."

"All blondes remind you of something."

"No, I'm serious. She says she's a waitress, but I keep thinking that I've seen her some place when she wasn't wearing an apron. But she's only lived here a few weeks and claims she knew Jeri only from passing her on the walk, which, incidentally, she did Tuesday evening about six-thirty. That seems to be the last anybody saw her alive."

Six-thirty Tuesday evening. Osgood looked at his watch again. It was now a few minutes past noon on Thursday, and by this time there was nothing to show for the tragedy in the bathroom except a ring around the tub and a fancy gown on the bed that wasn't going dancing any more. Even the curiosity seekers in the courtyard were thinning out now that the body was gone, and Frenchy's acrobatic eyebrows had a sort of why-don't-we-get-out-of-here? expression. Osgood wasn't going to give him a chance to ask the question, because he didn't have an answer. All he had was an uneasy feeling that something wasn't just the way it looked, and feelings couldn't be entered in a routine report.

But on the way to the door he scooped up a handful of those publicity stills from the desk drawer. On a dull day a city editor could make quite a spread out of a beautiful corpse in a bathtub no matter how she died. There was more than one way of locating the next of kin.

CHAPTER THREE

Although Wilma missed the excitement that only an amber-eyed cat watched from her garage-top vantage point, she didn't have to wait for the evening papers to hear of Jeri Lynn's fate. No sooner had the sound of sirens faded from the street than self-appointed couriers descended on the bakery in numbers—all asking for Wilma.

"Have you heard?" they all began, and then hastened on to repeat the story with colorful variations that always reached the same almost envious inquiry: "Isn't that the court where you live, Miss Rathjen? Isn't that your brother's place?" At first Wilma was terrified by all this unusual attention, and then she began to feel a heady importance. It became a great temptation to admit that she had known all about this exciting news long before they did; but, no, finger to the lips. Secrets could be exciting, too, and not nearly so dangerous.

"Jeri Lynn?" Waggoner echoed, after the fourth recital. "I've heard that name some place before."

"She was an actress," Wilma said.

"That wouldn't mean anything to me. The only actress's name I remember is Garbo, and I'm sure they didn't find her in your brother's bathtub."

Wilma started to protest that it wasn't really her brother's bathtub, but then she realized what was troubling Waggoner. She was jealous. All the customers wanted Wilma to wait on them now, and they bought much more than usual just in order to prolong the conversation. Why, at this rate the stock would be sold out before closing time! It was almost like being a celebrity.

And so Wilma began to feel very happy. Not because of the girl's death, of course, although she had surely brought down the wrath of God upon herself, but because this time she had been right. She hadn't imagined it after all; it really had happened. The dark images Ann Jenner had aroused in her mind the previous day faded to nothingness now. She wasn't going to be sick again. She wasn't going to be taken from her own lovely apartment and stripped of privacy and pride. The rain was gone, the sun was out, and the whole world seemed to be celebrating this singular victory with her. She began to plan what she would do tomorrow, her day off. Perhaps she would go to the library or on a walking tour of the shops. Ordinarily she would have taken in a downtown matinee, for Wilma, although she appreciated the intentions of those who disdained the movies because of their immoral content, believed that one should be aware of the evil in the world in order to be on guard against it. But this week there would be no matinee because of the price of that birthday cake. That was the one thing she still held against Jeri Lynn.

It was late afternoon when Wilma moved on to the next customer, after still another recitation of the neighborhood sensation, and found someone who wanted to hear the story rather than tell it. One glance at the white uniform across the counter and she reached for the raspberry tarts. Ann Jenner often came in at this hour and bought four tarts. She and Dr. Fergus shared an afternoon tea break whenever the doctor's schedule permitted.

"What were you saying about Jeri Lynn?" the nurse asked.

Wilma could hardly believe her ears. "Haven't you heard?" she asked. "The girl was found dead this morning, dead in her bath. They say she's been dead for at least two days."

The paper bags were on a table just behind the counter, and so Wilma didn't see Ann's initial reaction. But when she turned about again the nurse's face was as white as her uniform.

"Two days?" she echoed.

"That's what they say."

"Oh, no!"

The words were out before Ann could stop them. She looked frightened and stunned.

"Was Miss Lynn a particular friend of yours?" Wilma asked, but there was no reply. No answer, no question, no eager bending over the counter for details. On the contrary, Ann started to turn away.

"Miss Jenner, your tarts," Wilma called.

"Tarts?" She might just as well have said unicorns or gargoyles. "Oh, thank you."

"That will be thirty cents, please."

Unicorns, gargoyles, or mome raths. Eventually the woman did pay for the tarts, but her hands were trembling and cold as ice. Obviously, she'd been badly shaken by hearing of Jeri Lynn's death in so abrupt a manner, but Wilma wasn't particularly sorry. It was no more than what she deserved for spying on her upstairs neighbor. Still, it was a most peculiar reaction for a woman normally so self-possessed as Ann Jenner. Wilma thought about it for all of thirty seconds until the next customer arrived.

For the second evening in succession Wilma omitted the routine inspection of her apartment when she came home from work, and this time not from a greater fear but from an almost carefree lack of fear. It was as if the death of Jeri Lynn had driven off the cloud that seemed to be appearing in the distance. Now it was no cloud at all, only a mirage. Was the wing chair out of position? Were the shutter screens ajar? Had the magazines been displaced on the cobbler's bench? Ridiculous! Why should anyone enter her apartment? Why should anyone disturb her things or wear her clothes? She switched on the small table radio beside the wing chair and then turned it off again. The doctor had told her not to listen to the particular commentator she was about to hear, because his presentation was so alarming. This was nonsense, of course, for in such times as this, one should be alerted to the dangers within; but somehow Wilma didn't feel like being alarmed this evening. She felt like a hearty supper (too bad it had to be canned hash), some good music, and perhaps a little poetry from one of the thin volumes on the bookshelf. It had been like a spring day after the rain, and spring days made Wilma feel almost young again.

And spring evenings— She picked up the purring Alice and cradled the yellow cat in her arms. Spring evenings could be lonely.

But this particular evening was not destined to be lonely after all. Wilma had just finished her solitary meal and was clearing away the dishes when she caught sound of a familiar step on the stairs. There was no mistaking Curtis's step—quick and firm as if each one cost good money and he was determined to get full value for every expenditure. The step of a man who knows where he's going, Wilma always thought, and felt a swift surge of sisterly pride. Perhaps it was foolish to become so excited over a visit from her brother, but Wilma was flushed when she opened the door.

"Why, it's so nice to see you, Curtis," she cried. "It's been months! Did Katherine and the children come?"

Foolish question. Katherine and the children never came, but it always seemed more polite to ask. Curtis, however, didn't bother to answer. He came in without greeting or ceremony and didn't seem interested in unbuttoning his coat or removing his hat. One of the things Wilma admired about Curtis, when she was in such a mellow mood, was that he always wore a hat. So many men didn't any more.

A hat made him look taller and more distinguished. It also covered the place where his pale-gold hair had thinned to the point of extinction. Curtis wasn't an old man—he was two years younger than Wilma, and she was only forty-three no matter what the mirror claimed—but his hair had been thinning for about the same length of time his waistline had been expanding. Wilma, of course, seldom noticed these things. She seldom had the chance.

For a few moments he stood motionless just inside the door, staring at his sister as if reading a weather warning. Fair and moderate, it seemed to report, and Curtis was visibly relieved.

"I know it's been a long time," he said at last. "I've been intending to stop by, but I've been so busy lately."

"Oh, I know!" Wilma responded. "I saw your picture in the paper yesterday. Miss Jenner brought it to my attention."

Mentioning Ann Jenner's name was deliberate. Curtis was no actor. If he had put the nurse up to watching her and reporting on her actions, the guilt would show on his face. But the only thing showing was a marked lack of interest.

"The nurse in the north front unit," she prompted, and Curtis nodded vaguely.

"Oh," he said. "Well, no matter. What I came to see you about is this terrible business downstairs. I wanted to make sure you were all right, Wil'."

"But of course I'm all right, Curtis. Why shouldn't I be?"

"I mean, you're not upset or anything?"

Wilma had difficulty smothering her smile. She might have known that Curtis had a reason for paying her this visit. The story of Jeri Lynn's death was in all the papers now, and Curtis never understood, any more than anyone else ever understood, that evil uncovered didn't disturb her; only evil that remained hidden.

"Why should I be upset?" she chided. "My conscience is clear."

"Conscience? Hang it all, Wil', what's this poor girl's death got to do with anyone's conscience?"

Wilma started to answer and then pressed her thin lips together. She would speak no evil of the dead. Jeri Lynn, or whatever her real name might have been, had gone on to a higher judgment than her own. She would pay for her wantonness without mortal condemnation. But she could at least warn Curtis against another act of folly.

"I do hope you'll be more careful about renting the place again," she said. "Try to get some nice, respectable person."

"What was wrong with Jeri Lynn?" Curtis snapped.

"What was wrong—" Wilma held back her words. It was a trap. Curtis expected her to come out with some lurid tale, which, of course, he wouldn't believe, but she'd learned better than to reveal everything she knew. "I didn't say there was anything wrong with her," she added quickly, "but show people are so inconsiderate. Noisy, careless with the furnishings, and you're never sure of getting the rent money. Why, I doubt if Jeri Lynn put in half a dozen days' work in all the months I've been here!"

As careful as she'd been, Wilma knew that she'd said something wrong. She could tell by the two bright-pink spots that suddenly appeared in her brother's round cheeks. He began to look very grave.

"Have you been talking to the police?" he demanded.

"Why, no— Do you think I shall have to?"

Now Curtis looked relieved. "No, I don't think so. If they haven't been around by this time, they'll probably leave you alone. But if they should come, or if any newspaper reporters come around, be careful of what you say. Understand?"

"But, Curtis, what could I say?"

"That's what worries me. God only knows!"

Curtis strode over to the windows and looked out upon the flat roofs below. For a moment Wilma was terrified lest he notice that one bright window of Jeri Lynn's apartment; and then she remembered that the window was no longer bright, for the apartment was dark and empty now.

"What you just said about Miss Lynn not working would be enough," he muttered. "It's talk like that that starts trouble, and there's nothing to it. You're all wrong about that girl, Wilma. She just had a bad break."

Now that Curtis wasn't watching, Wilma smiled openly. Her brother could be awfully naïve.

"Why, when Jeri rented that apartment she had a wonderful job," he added. "She was featured in the floor show at a little club down the street, and talent scouts were hot on her heels. But then she got sick and had to quit."

"Is that what she told you?"

Curtis swung about and met Wilma's challenge with a glare. "She didn't have to tell me, I was here! I was on the premises the night she collapsed. I was present when the doctor arrived, and I heard him tell her she was overworked and would have to take a rest. That was six months or so ago, before you came here. Naturally, it was hard to get started again."

"And who paid her rent for six months?"

It was much too late for Curtis to realize that he'd talked himself into a corner. The pink spots on his cheeks were momentarily scarlet, and for just an instant Wilma felt a surge of incredible fear, incredible because this was Curtis, her brother. Then the anger faded into submission.

"No one," he said. "But what was I to do, throw her out in the street? I felt sorry for the kid."

It wasn't like Curtis to allow sympathy to interfere with business—and rightly so, Wilma believed. Letting Wallace Timm work out part of his rent was a different story; a handy man and gardener would have cost more than his gratuity. But Jeri Lynn! How could that girl have worked out her keep? The thought left Wilma momentarily stunned, and then she shuddered. What was she thinking? This was Curtis, a fine husband and father, a leader of the community!

"For heaven's sake, Wil', don't look so shocked," he said. "It was just a temporary arrangement. A girl in that profession may have a spotty income while she's getting started, but once she clicks—"

"Then it was just a loan," Wilma cried eagerly.

"Of course it was! I had a lot of faith in that girl. But you can see how careless talk could create a wrong impression. That's why you've got to watch yourself."

Curtis had removed his hat in these last few moments and was twisting it about in his hands like some small boy in trouble. Wilma remembered quite suddenly that she was the elder. Papa had been gone almost twenty years, and Mamma—was it already two? She was the elder. She wanted to push back Curtis's hair from his forehead, just as she had done so many times in the years long gone; but now he was himself again, the hat went back in place.

"By the way, Wil'," he added, easing over toward the door, "I'd just as soon you didn't mention any of this to Katherine. You know how wives are?"

How can I mention anything to Katherine when I never see her? Wilma thought. *And how could I know how wives are?* But she promised just the same. It was difficult not to promise anything to Curtis. And now he could be on his way again. A committee meeting was waiting somewhere, or a banquet, or some big deal. His departing footsteps on the stairs were eager and jaunty, like those of a salesman who has just sold a tough client. From the front windows Wilma watched him follow the narrow walk out to the street, and then listened for the familiar roar of a high-powered motor. Curtis was gone and so was her happiness. So that was why he had come!

She turned about slowly, aware of a familiar chilling sensation. It wasn't a spring evening any more, and her lovely room seemed strange and hostile. The wing chair—had she mussed the cushions that way? And whose dirty shoes had been tracking up her rug?

"No, I won't look!" she cried aloud. "I won't see the things that aren't there!"

To make certain, she switched off the lights.

It was a quarter past twelve by the illuminated clock on the New Salem desk when Alice began to protest. She had waited patiently while her mistress dozed in the arm-chair, but there came a time when any-well-bred feline must demand attention. Heaven be praised, the woman was aroused at last! A few more yowls and she made it to the door.

The first thing Wilma noticed when she stepped outside was how the wind had risen. It was always stronger on the roof than anywhere else, but tonight it was a wild, gusty creature that swept across the city like a lover bearing great armfuls of gathered-up scents: the rain-washed hills, the spicy eucalyptus, the heavy sweetness of the night-blooming jasmine—and something else. She moved closer to the porch railing and breathed in deeply. A cigarette. Someone was smoking in the courtyard below. She listened, but there were no voices. She strained her eyes at the darkness, glad now that she'd come out without switching on the lights, and finally found one shadow that was different from the rest. Once she caught the red glow of the cigarette, but the shadow (it was impossible to determine its sex) was facing the rear wall of the south bungalow.

But that was Jeri Lynn's apartment! Wilma strained for-ward, looking where the shadow looked and seeing, even-tually, what the shadow saw. It came intermittently, a moving ball of light that showed first at one window and then another, and then at times became a prodding finger that searched silently through the dead woman's apartment. Fascinated, Wilma watched both the light and the shadow. Once the shadow half-turned, and she thought then that it was a policeman who stood in the courtyard. But what could the police be searching for at this hour, and why would they use a torch instead of turning on the lights? Before she could think of an answer, a sudden gust of wind caught the screen door behind her and slammed it back against the wall like the crack of a starting gun. For an instant the shadow had a white face, then it was gone, and an echo of running footsteps faded down the driveway.

A searcher inside, a nervous watcher outside— The light disappeared from the windows, and Wilma was alone with her puzzle at midnight.

CHAPTER FOUR

As Osgood anticipated, the press found space for Jeri Lynn. Any girl that beautiful wasn't going to die in so unorthodox a manner without a picture spread that would have quickened the heart of her agent had the lady been in any condition to sign on the dotted line. But despite all the publicity, it was midmorning of the following day before anything developed. The phone call was very mysterious.

"It's something about that girl you found dead in the bathtub," the woman said. "No, I can't tell you now. This is a business phone, and the line has to be kept open. And I don't want any policemen hanging around the counter scaring off trade. I'll meet you in the parking lot at noon."

That, and the address of a market out on Santa Monica

Boulevard, was the size of it. It sounded like a waste of time, but the citizens had to be served.

It was about five minutes of twelve when Frenchy parked the sedan in the big double parking lot, and that gave Osgood just enough time to make that daily call home from a public booth at the driveway. While calling, he could gaze out on the faces of the smiling ladies on La Rene's billboards, and they weren't exactly strangers. La Rene ran too lively a place not to be well known to the police. By the time Osgood returned to the sedan with an order for a loaf of wheat-germ bread tucked under his fedora, Frenchy was talking to a pudgy little woman in the back seat. One look at her and Osgood thought the bakery must have instituted a mental-telepathy order service.

"This is Mrs. Waggoner, the lady who called in about Jeri Lynn," Frenchy began, but it wasn't Frenchy's story, and that little woman in the back seat wasn't going to share her big moment with any gabby policeman.

"I read all about her in the papers," she said quickly. "I would have called sooner, but everything was in such a mess this morning—" She paused and patted her sweaty face with a wadded handkerchief. It wasn't that warm, but Leota Waggoner was excited. "Every time she closes the store it's a mess the next day," she added petulantly. "None of the help they send me these days is any good, but Wilma Rathjen is the worst yet!"

"And who," Osgood sighed, "is Wilma Rathjen?"

"My helper, the one who sold the birthday cake to the dead girl."

Let there be a sensational story in the news and all sorts of queer characters crawled out from under the rocks to sun themselves in the light of publicity. Osgood glanced at Frenchy, and Frenchy shook his head, but nothing was going to discourage this moon-faced little bakery manager with the snapping eyes and wagging tongue.

"Birthday cakes are a special order," she explained.

"What I mean is that they have to be ordered ahead of time for delivery on the date the customer specifies. Well, this dead girl, Jeri Lynn, ordered the five-ninety-five special last week, and it was to be delivered Wednesday. That's the day before yesterday."

Osgood knew perfectly well what day it was, and he was getting restless. "What are we supposed to do?" he muttered. "Pay for it?"

"Oh, it's paid for. It was picked up and paid for on the date of delivery."

Mrs. Waggoner paused as if waiting for an offstage fanfare. The pause gave time for her declaration to sink in, and an itching of curiosity began to replace Osgood's boredom.

"Who picked it up?" he asked.

"The customer, I presume. At least that's what Miss Rathjen told me when I asked her about it Wednesday afternoon."

Osgood didn't have a trumpet for the fanfare, but there was nothing wrong with his arithmetic. If Jeri Lynn ran that fatal bath Tuesday evening, she would have had a little difficulty picking up an order at the bakery the following afternoon. He remarked on that discrepancy, and the woman in the back seat nodded as if her head were attached by spring steel.

"I know," she said brightly. "It said in my paper that she'd been dead for about two days, but I couldn't get it out of my mind that I'd seen or heard her name somewhere before. This morning I went through the old orders and found this." She passed a small slip of paper across the back of the seat, and Osgood and Frenchy scrutinized the order sheet for one four-layer special with chocolate icing, pink sugar roses, and the inscription: *Happy Birthday Darling*. The customer's name and the date of delivery—Wednesday, February 17—verified everything she had said.

"What I've been asking myself," Mrs. Waggoner added thoughtfully, "is how this girl could come into the store, pay for her cake, and take it home, and all the time be lying dead in her bathtub."

The question the woman posed was of sufficient validity to incur a speculative silence. The cause of Jeri Lynn's death was too obvious to require a complete autopsy; but the medic's report bore out the testimony of the tenants at the court as to the approximate time of her electrocution, and this was no minor deviation that Mrs. Waggoner had suggested. There must be some simple explanation.

"Maybe it was another Jeri Lynn," Osgood suggested, but Mrs. Waggoner shook her head.

"It's the same one, all right. Why, she lives right in the very court where Wilma Rathjen lives! She knew the girl by sight."

"And does she say it was Jeri Lynn who picked up that cake?"

"I haven't asked her. This is her day off."

Osgood caught Frenchy's eye and held back a smile. It looked as if he'd been right in the first place, and all this excitement was for nothing. The mystery wasn't such a mystery after all if the saleslady who made the transaction hadn't seen fit to call the police. Anybody could have picked up that order in the dead girl's place— But then the smile, died again, because he was only trading puzzles. If someone had claimed Jeri Lynn's birthday cake, the very act suggested a couple of interesting thoughts such as who did it and why.

"Rathjen—" Frenchy murmured. "It seems that I've heard that name before."

"You've probably heard of her brother, Curtis Rathjen," Mrs. Waggoner suggested. "He's in the news every now and then."

It so happened that Osgood was watching Frenchy's face when this bit of information broke, and along with the swift dismay and elevated eyebrows he could almost hear the bells ringing. The memory of Frenchy Bartel was phenomenal. Whenever he associated a name and a recollection, it was dead certain to be correct. In this instance it seemed to be a pretty painful association that grew even more painful with the woman's unsolicited commentary.

"You might think a man that well off would at least look after his own sister instead of wishing her off on me," she muttered. "Honestly, I sometimes doubt that the woman's all there!"

"Oh, no!" Frenchy groaned. "Not that again!"

It was at least five minutes before Osgood could get Leota Waggoner headed back to her realm of pies and pastries and get at the reason for Frenchy's outburst. Whatever had started those bells ringing wasn't for the benefit of neighborhood gossip, and so, with profuse thanks for her good citizenship and the promise that her suspicions would be investigated, he sent her swishing off with a curiosity as big as his own and twice as imaginative. Frenchy could be imaginative, too, on occasion, but it wasn't imagination that had put all that grief in his big brown eyes.

"Who is Curtis Rathjen?" Osgood asked, as soon as the woman was out of earshot.

Frenchy's grief mingled with amazement. "Don't you ever buy a newspaper?"

"Certainly. How else could I line the garbage pail?"

Because Osgood wasn't much for following social and civic affairs, he had to get the picture of Curtis Rathjen from a man with bitter memories. It was a familiar picture. Rathjen had started small and by hard work, initiative, and the stimulant a few wars can give to land values, had reached the place where he could be called a self-made man without creating hard feelings. Frenchy painted him as a pillar of society: service clubs, charities, politics.

"So?" Osgood prodded.

"So his sister is a nut. Listen, Johnny, about a year ago I was working a night detail across town, and complaints kept coming in about a prowler who was disturbing the citizens in a certain residential district. We did a little prowling of our own one night and caught the culprit in the act, but what do you think? Instead of the usual Peeping Tom, it turned out to be a skinny little woman about forty or forty-five years old. She seemed harmless enough when we pulled her out of the hedges, but when the citizen she was watching came out of the house, she began screaming he was a spy with a direct radio beam to Moscow! Come to find out, the poor fellow was a schoolteacher who liked to play with his son's chemical set and had installed his own TV antenna because he couldn't afford a professional."

"Did he lose his job?" Osgood asked.

"I don't know, but I do know that the old girl lost her head when we tried to talk her out of the idea. She thought I was a gangster trying to make a snatch, I had to fast-talk her into thinking we were from the F.B.I. just to get her down to the station! Like I said before, she's a nut."

"Garden variety," Osgood muttered.

"Sure, I'll grant you they're cropping up like ragweed after the rains, but not all of them have a Brother Curtis, praise the Lord! Brother Curtis is a little sensitive about having a screwball sister. What I mean is, he doesn't like having lowly police sergeants nosing around and stirring up publicity. He got to the station with a psychiatrist and a court order before the ink was dry on the blotter. Wilma went off to a nice, secluded sanitarium, and it was nip and tuck for a while as to whether or not I was going off to the hills."

Frenchy leaned back in the seat and frowned at the toes of his suede moccasins, while Osgood pondered the problem. As the situation now stood, they had a simple case of accidental death with no questions asked and no irate citizens to placate. If nobody showed up to claim the body, Jeri Lynn would get a cheap funeral and quick oblivion. If they nosed around and stirred up a hornet's nest (Osgood had mixed with many a Curtis Rathjen), it probably wouldn't change the situation anyway. Wilma Rathjen, if she was anything like Frenchy's report, could have sold that cake to anyone and never known the difference; as for that bakery manager, anyone with half an eye could see that she belonged on the back fence with the rest of the cats.

But nineteen years was a long time to play guardian to the blindfolded lady. A man got to the place where he looked for trouble in the most peculiar places, and found it in the strangest things! A birthday cake! It was as crazy a clue as Osgood had run across in many a year. How could there be anything suspicious about Jeri Lynn's death? Call it careless, call it stupid, but how could anyone call it murder?

And yet, just thinking back to the dead girl's apartment with everything just as it had been when they found her a scant twenty-four hours earlier, he began to feel again that sense of something wrong—something not quite the way it seemed to be—

"I warn you," Frenchy said, reading in advance the decision on Osgood's face, "the old girl doesn't like policemen after what happened that night. I'll never forget the way she glared at me when she found out the desk sergeant wasn't J. Edgar Hoover!"

"You can sit in the car," Osgood muttered. "I'll get around her some way."

But Frenchy didn't have to worry. They had to drive west along the boulevard a bit before reaching that side street lined with old bungalow courts, and a couple of blocks down the line Osgood noticed a canopy over one of the shops that made everything wonderfully clear. Now he knew what it was that had been bothering him ever since the girls next door trooped into the dead girl's apartment to tell their stories, and it meant that Frenchy didn't have to waste the taxpayers' money by sitting in the car while he talked shop to a scatterbrained bakery clerk. Frenchy could drive back up on the boulevard and have a little talk with whoever operated Elaine's Beauty Parlor. It seemed that an establishment like that should furnish its own hair dryers.

CHAPTER FIVE

Wilma usually slept late on her day off—sometimes as late as nine or nine-thirty—but after that frightening experience on the roof she had trouble sleeping at all. Her first thought had been to call Curtis, but that would never do. She would arouse the whole household at that hour, and Katherine would be angry again. She knew exactly how Katherine felt about her—annoyed, almost afraid. It was foolish for anyone to be afraid of a woman who was herself so afraid of everyone, but sometimes it amused Wilma to think of Katherine being afraid of her. Amusing or not, however, calling Curtis was out of the question. He would only think she had been imagining things again.

And so she had gone to bed to wrestle fitfully with her pillow and the parade of terrible dreams that began whenever sleep crept in. Morning came like Easter tidings, and Wilma resurrected her weary mind and body from the tortures of darkness. It would be another day of sunshine, and she would feel better. Perhaps she really had imagined the prowler and the watcher after all.

Morning was the quietest time of day at the court. The tenants were either at work or still asleep, and for a few hours Wilma had the place to herself. Once she caught a glimpse of Wallace Timm crossing the courtyard with a ladder under his arm, but there was no other activity, and in the midst of all that quiet she began to think of the prowler again. Perhaps someone else had seen him, too. The comings and goings never seemed to stop around the court. But when she looked for the old man again, intending to call down and ask him in some indirect manner, there was no sign of the man. The wide cement driving area in front of the garage was deserted, and the tiny patches of earth around the units were not being raked or trimmed. It was then that curiosity got the better of Wilma. She seldom ventured below into the tenants' domain, but this was a special occasion. Moments later she was trotting down the stairs to inspect the narrow flower beds outside Jeri Lynn's kitchen and bathroom windows.

The recent rain had left the earth damp enough to retain footprints, but on this score Wilma was disappointed. No footprints, no crushed lilies, no trampled grass. She was almost relieved. It was much easier to write off the prowlers as just another bad dream. But as she stepped back, still with her eyes cast down, an object on the cement came into view. It was a cigarette butt with a long ash, as if it had been thrown away to burn itself out rather than been crushed under foot. As she picked up the unburned remainder, Wilma couldn't help remembering how that white-faced shadow had fled at the sound of the screen door behind him. No time, surely, for grinding out his cigarette.

"Well, good morning, Miss Rathjen. Your day off?"

Wilma straightened up and whirled about angrily. It was a terrible thing to be accosted from behind, especially when one was engaged in the questionable act of retrieving a cigarette butt. She might have known it would be Ruby Lennox. That woman had no sense of propriety whatsoever.

"You're up early today, Miss Lennox," Wilma said acidly. It was all of ten o'clock, but Ruby didn't recognize an insult when she heard one.

"Yeah, I couldn't sleep," she answered. "I guess that business with the kid across the way bothered me more than I thought. I couldn't sleep worth a damn. Gotta match, honey? Oh, that's right, you don't smoke, do you? I keep forgetting you don't smoke."

For a moment Wilma was afraid that Ruby had seen the cigarette butt she was so carefully hiding from view and was being sarcastic; but apparently that wasn't the case. From one of the pockets of the coolie coat Ruby had withdrawn a crumpled cigarette and was now searching the same pocket for a match. Fumbling was a better word for it. Even to one totally unfamiliar with the symptoms it was obvious that the woman must be suffering from a hang-over. Her short silver-blond hair was a tousled mop, and her face was of a color not unlike left-over cream gravy. The hours between dusk and dawn always had a devastating effect on Ruby's beauty.

"The poor kid," she muttered, "You heard about it, I guess."

"I heard," Wilma said.

"How do you like that? Just a kid and she passes out without a soul knowin'. Christ, I'd have figured any one of us would get out ahead of her!"

It might have been an accident that Ruby sounded as if Jeri Lynn had broken jail. Perhaps life could seem that way on a dismal morning after; she didn't elaborate. Without a match the cigarette was no good. It went back into her pocket.

"Were you lookin' for somethin'?" she asked, and Wilma quickly assumed the air of the landlord's crotchety sister.

"I thought I saw Mr. Timm down here awhile ago. I had a little chore for him to do."

"He oughta be around here somewhere. He always is." Ruby squinted at the sunlight and shuddered. "Maybe this is the day he collects his unemployment insurance.

Christ, I gotta do something for this head! Did you ever feel like you were locked up in a runaway freight car? I need a hair from the dog that bit me!"

Wilma wasn't quite sure what the woman was talking about, but she was relieved when she stumbled back inside her own apartment and brought the unpleasantness to an end. Talking to Ruby Lennox was a disgusting experience under any circumstances, and just now Wilma had something important to do. She ran quickly up the stairs to her own small sanctuary, and there, safely away from uninvited eyes, examined the cigarette butt. She had seen detectives in films deduce all manner of facts from such a clue; but all she could make of it was that it was one of the more common brands advertised so disgustingly by every medium, and that it bore no trace of lipstick. Not much to go on, surely, and yet it came as welcome reassurance. A man had stood in the dark courtyard below and watched the light inside Jeri Lynn's apartment. By such simple evidence this was now fact and not fancy.

Fact, not fancy. The thought wouldn't go away. Wilma tried to busy herself with other things, but the puzzle of the night prowlers would return and leave her standing in the center of the room with a broom in her hands that she couldn't remember having taken from the closet, or a pan of suds in the sink for the dishes she'd washed hours ago. What had that man in the courtyard been doing there? Why had someone with a flashlight searched the dead girl's apartment? She knew that she was incapable of solving the puzzle alone; but now that she had evidence, Curtis wouldn't laugh at her. As owner of the property, he was certainly entitled to know. What's more, now that she thought about it, now that she remembered certain things, it seemed that Curtis might be very interested in knowing.

It was almost noon when Wilma ventured out of her

apartment again. Despite the hour, the court was still quiet. By this time the theatricals should have been playing ballet music on the record player or sunning themselves on the porch; Ruby Lennox should have had the radio serials going full blast; and Tony Carmen should have been out in his swimming trunks polishing down his long convertible. The very unnaturalness of the place encouraged her suspicion that something was wrong; and so delicate a matter couldn't be discussed over a party line. Wilma's destination was the public phone booth up on the boulevard; but as she came down the center walk an unexpected sight met her eyes—Curtis's car! He was already here! As she stood under the stucco archway pondering this situation, the back door of the big sedan swung open and revealed a three-foot spaceman armed with a deathray gun and a Hopalong Cassidy accent.

"Stick 'em up," bawled the spaceman, "or I'll blast you off Terra!"

Under the circumstances, this would have been comparatively easy, and then Wilma regained her senses enough to recognize a small boy's face behind the plastic helmet. Curtis had a strict rule against tenants with children—that's why he preferred unmarried people—but this child looked familiar. Then she noticed the medical insignia on the car.

"Why, you're Doctor Fergus's little boy, aren't you?" she said. "Is your father inside?"

The child responded with a steady blue-eyed stare as he trained the ray gun on Wilma's head.

"Is someone ill? Is Miss Jenner home today?"

Standing with her back to the nurse's doorway, she couldn't see when the door opened behind her. The first indication she had of an eavesdropper came by way of a terse command.

"Donnie, stop that! Put that pistol down and get back in the car!"

Wilma whirled about. A tall young man with tired eyes stood in the doorway of Ann Jenner's apartment. Arnold Fergus was a familiar figure in the neighborhood, particularly, Wilma reflected, in the vicinity of Ann Jenner's apartment. Something of what she was thinking must have crept into her eyes, because the doctor regarded her coldly.

"Did you wish to see me, Miss Rathjen?" he asked.

Later Wilma would recall that the doctor used her name in spite of the fact that they had never been introduced; but at the moment she was aware of nothing except an unreasonable sense of panic.

"Why, no," she stammered. "I was just wondering if Miss Jenner is all right."

"Why shouldn't she be?"

Wilma blinked rapidly. "I really don't know; but yesterday—"

"What about yesterday?"

At first Wilma had thought the doctor looked tired, as well he might with his flourishing practice; but now he seemed both tired and angry. Perhaps he didn't like being caught at Ann Jenner's apartment. There was nothing wrong with it, of course. She was his nurse, and he was (as Ann Jenner surely knew) an eligible young widower with a small son; but because of the anger Wilma decided not to mention the nurse's strange reaction to the news of Jeri Lynn's death. "Perhaps it was the day before yesterday," she corrected, "I don't remember exactly when I saw her, but she mentioned something about all the flu going around. I was just wondering—I mean, after seeing your car—"

"Oh, I see."

Some people took Wilma Rathjen to be a terrible fool. As if she couldn't see the swift relief flooding the young man's eyes. "As a matter of fact," he said quickly, "that is why I'm here. Miss Jenner's running a slight temperature.

I just dropped by on my lunch hour to see how she's getting along."

"Oh, I'm sorry," Wilma said. "Is there anything I can do?"

It seemed only polite to ask. There was no call for the doctor to react so abruptly.

"I'm sure Miss Jenner can take care of herself," he snapped. "Donnie, I told you to get back in the car!" The child scurried for the sedan, and the door of Ann's apartment slammed shut like an exclamation point. It was all very strange. Medical men were usually better mannered than young Dr. Fergus, and Wilma was still smarting under the rebuff as she hurried off down the street. So Ann Jenner wasn't feeling well! She could commit no such unchristian act as to wish sickness on the girl, but it did seem a kind of justice that this inquisitive creature should be struck down by the same claim she had tried to attribute to her neighbor. Despite Curtis's lack of response when she mentioned the nurse last night, Wilma still hadn't forgotten her fright the evening Ann drove her home. The girl was too nosy for her own good. It served her right to be sick!

But then Wilma began to wonder. Ann Jenner was a very healthy young woman—was it coincidence that she'd taken ill so soon after hearing of Jeri Lynn's death? And what was the girl to her that she should be so upset at the news of what had happened in that bathroom? They seemed rarely to speak to one another. Certainly there was nothing in common between a beautiful, fun-loving entertainer and a drab, hard-working nurse! And then, through an unheard din of traffic noise as she neared the boulevard, Wilma seemed to hear Curtis telling her again about the night Jeri Lynn had collapsed and he'd been with her when the doctor arrived. But what doctor? And what nurse?

From even the weakest chain of circumstance Wilma could

build a shackle of fear. A searching light in a dead girl's apartment—a cigarette butt on the cement drive—a nurse who seemed as healthy as a channel swimmer until the last time she'd come to the bakery for raspberry tarts—. So many strange things had happened since Jeri Lynn died. Why should that unhappy event cause so many unusual reactions? Wilma waited at the intersection for the lights to change, and then, quite suddenly, it seemed that she knew.

There would be no call to Curtis. The lights changed three times before Wilma regained her senses enough to turn around and head back to the bungalow court. She mustn't run. She mustn't do anything to attract attention, because she'd done too much already! There was only one reason for all these strange happenings: Jeri Lynn had been murdered, and all these people knew! Ann Jenner, Dr. Fergus, the prowlers—they must all know that something was wrong with that accident. And Curtis? The thought of Curtis made her break into a trot in spite of the determination not to run, because Curtis had spared some of his valuable time to come to see her on the very night the girl's body had been found. Curtis was suspicious. What wouldn't he think if he should come back and find that birthday cake on the top of her refrigerator!

Wilma was too excited by the time she reached the court to notice either the absence of Dr. Fergus's big sedan or the return of normalcy to the courtyard. Tony Carmen was out in his skintight trunks, the theatricals' record player was going at full volume, and Ruby Lennox was listening to the radio serials; but all Wilma was aware of was the baffling problem of how to dispose of an object too large for the garbage pail and too conspicuous for the trash. She should have got rid of it under cover of darkness, of course, but there was something about that ornate confection that still troubled her. Something wrong—something she felt responsible for. But now she would have to get rid of it even if it entailed acute indigestion.

Ignoring Tony's teasing wolf whistle, she hurried up the center walk and ran up her own flight of stairs—only to be brought up short by the sight of an unexpected invasion. A man, an entirely unfamiliar man, was sitting very calmly in her deck chair and stroking Alice's back.

CHAPTER SIX

"Miss Rathjen?" The man asked, and Wilma gripped the stair rail for much needed support. "I hope you'll excuse my waiting like this, but they told me you'd probably just stepped out to the market and would be right back."

Wilma finally found a voice but not a very strong one. "They?" she repeated.

"Some girls I met in the courtyard downstairs. They suggested that I wait. Lovely view you have here."

Wilma had never considered the view except as a vantage point for watching other peoples' lives; it was rather surprising to hear a collection of flat roofs and ragged hills referred to in that way. But aside from being a stranger and unexpected, there was nothing particularly alarming about the man. He looked neat and respectable—probably a salesman of some kind, and Alice seemed quite fond of him. He had got up from the deck chair the instant Wilma came into view, but the cat was still busily engaged in transferring yellow hairs to his trouser legs. Alice's opinion of people meant a great deal to Wilma.

"You wanted to see me?" she asked, and the man nodded.

"I'm Sergeant— I mean, I'm Mr. Sergeant. I represent an insurance company."

Wilma had to force back a smile. From the hesitant way in which he represented himself, Mr. Sergeant must be a very new agent. And he did seem such an earnest man, too.

"I'm sorry," she said, "but my brother handles all my insurance needs."

"No, you don't understand. I'm not selling insurance, Miss Rathjen. I'm just trying to get a little information about a client of ours. I thought you might have known her—Jeri Lynn."

Wilma was extracting the key from her handbag when this bombshell landed. At the sound of the girl's name, the key slipped from her hand and rang out like a small bell on the cement sun deck. The stranger found it for her under the chair.

"But she—" Wilma gasped.

"—is dead," the man said. "That's why I'm here."

"To investigate her death?"

Key in hand, Sergeant Osgood paused to study Wilma's stricken face. The play-acting was Frenchy's idea. "It figures," he insisted, as they had driven toward the court. "Anyone crazy enough to think a teacher is a Commie spy and a policeman is a gangster, won't doubt for a minute that you're an insurance man. That way you'll get to talk to her before she screams for Brother Curtis." Osgood didn't think much of the idea himself. He liked to show his credentials, introduce himself, and just get to work. But now he began to think that Frenchy was right. Wilma Rathjen looked normal enough, neat, simply dressed, certainly not like the obvious characters who could be seen any day parading the streets like a road, company of *The Snake Pit*. But now, at the mere mention of Jeri Lynn's name, she came out with the strangest question.

"Investigate?" he echoed. "Is there something about Miss Lynn's death that hasn't come to light?"

"There must be," Wilma said. "Otherwise you wouldn't be calling on me."

It was time for Osgood to start talking fast, but Osgood didn't know how to talk fast. He got busy with the key and had the door open before she could stop him. If this woman was crazy, he didn't want to match wits with a quiz kid!

"As a matter of fact," he muttered, "I do have a few questions. May I come in?"

It was safe to ask the question since he was already inside and much too big to be ejected by anything so small as this little woman with troubled eyes. What Osgood didn't realize, of course, was that the cause of the trouble in her eyes—as well as the cause of his unscheduled visit—was sitting in a cardboard box on the refrigerator. But Osgood didn't get that far. He got only as far as the living-room, and there he had to pause and collect his wits. After all he'd heard from Frenchy, he was prepared for any kind of witch's den up to and including a steaming caldron and a bevy of bats. He was not prepared for what he found. Small as it was, the apartment was tastefully decorated and spotlessly clean. The honey maple gleamed, the milk glass shone, and the gay chintz was as bright as the day of purchase. It was enough to make a man doubt his wits, or at least question the fabulous memory of Frenchy Bartel.

"I'm afraid you'll have to excuse the muss," Wilma said. "I haven't done much cleaning today. Won't you sit down, Mr. Sergeant?"

Osgood could find no muss, but he did find a wonderfully comfortable wing chair facing the wide front windows. From that vantage point nothing was visible outside except the tops of the highest palms that lined the parkway and a spread of blue sky. The rest of the court seemed a world away, and Jeri Lynn's missing birthday cake was like some joker's prank.

But now the woman was staring at him in a way that suggested he'd better concoct a convincing story.

"I suppose that you knew Miss Lynn," he began.

Wilma kept right on with her staring. "I've seen her

coming and going," she said.

"Do you recall the last time you saw her?"

"The last time?" Wilma's mouth worked nervously. She could have been trying to remember or trying to forget. "I suppose I saw her just about every day," she said at last, "so it must have been Monday. Monday evening, that is. She was never up when I left for work in the morning."

"Are you sure it was Monday?"

"Well, as I said, it must have been Monday. I didn't get home from the store until after seven Tuesday, and by that time she was—" Wilma broke off abruptly. Now she had trouble meeting Osgood's eyes. "According to the newspapers, Miss Lynn died Tuesday night," she added quickly. "I didn't see her then, so it must have been Monday."

"The newspapers only know what the police tell them," Osgood remarked, "and the police only tell what they want to tell. But I'll explain what this is all about. What I'm trying to do is to establish the exact time of Miss Lynn's death."

"Is that important?"

"To my company, yes. You see, Miss Lynn was behind in her premiums and the period of grace expired at midnight Tuesday. If she died before midnight, as everyone seems to think, then we're stuck with a claim. But if she died after midnight, well, you can see what I mean."

Osgood paused to see how Wilma was taking the story. For sheer improvisation it wasn't so bad. He felt pretty proud of himself. But nothing happened.

"If she was seen alive any time after midnight," he added hopefully, "on Wednesday, let's say, then my company is in the clear."

The door was now wide open for the woman to walk in with an explanation for that missing birthday cake, but she didn't react according to plan. She sat upright on the edge of a small cricket chair and studied his face as intently as a victim trying to identify a suspect in a police line-up. He could see that it was going to take more than a gentle prod to get anything out of Wilma Rathjen.

"Wednesday," he repeated significantly. "You work at a bakery, don't you, Miss Rathjen?"

Her eyes brightened momentarily. "Yes," she said.

"A bakery in the big market up on the boulevard. I know that because I've just been up there talking to the manager of that bakery, and she told me a strange story about a birthday cake that Miss Lynn ordered last week. She says that the cake was delivered and called for on Wednesday, and that you handled the sale. Now how could that be, Miss Rathjen?"

Wilma's face never had much color. When she paled it wasn't too noticable, and she'd been growing paler from the first mention of the cake. Her eyes sought out a point beyond Osgood's shoulder; but even if he had followed the direction of her gaze, he wouldn't have seen what she was thinking about. The shutter screens blocked the view into the kitchen.

"Oh, that!" she said, at last. "I'd forgotten all about it. It didn't seem important."

"Not even when you heard that Miss Lynn was supposed to have died the night before?"

"Oh, I didn't sell the cake to Miss Lynn! How could I? It was someone else, a friend of hers."

"Someone you knew?"

Wilma didn't hesitate. One lie always made the next lie easier—and inevitable. "No, I'd never seen him before," she said. "He just came up to the counter and said he was to pick up an order for Miss Lynn. I didn't think anything about it. That sort of thing happens all the time."

Osgood leaned forward. "Can you describe this man?"

Describe him? Why not? Wilma's face twisted into a frown as if trying to recall important details.

"He was young," she said. "Older than Miss Lynn, but younger than you. And he was tall—but maybe not so tall as you. I couldn't see much of his face, because it was raining that day and he wore his hat turned down all the way around and his coat collar turned up. It was a raincoat. A tan raincoat."

"Could you identify him if you saw him again?"

The lie had to stop somewhere. Wilma sucked on her lower lip for a moment and then shook her head. "It was late in the afternoon when everybody comes in at once. I'm afraid there were just too many customers around, Mr. Sergeant. Is it so important?"

"I'm afraid," Osgood sighed, "it's just a false alarm."

Amid all this double-barreled deception, at least, the sigh was genuine. For a time back in the sedan when Mrs. Waggoner was spinning her unusual tale, he'd felt a twinge of excitement as if they were getting the scent of something after all. There were a couple of things that bothered him about Jeri Lynn's accident: the hair dryer and that dress spread out on her bed. She had a dinner date every night, the girls next door had said, but what kind of a date was it who wouldn't check up when his girl failed to show for two nights? A tall man in a tan raincoat!

Jeri Lynn must have known dozens of tall men with tan raincoats. But then Osgood hit on an idea that started him talking to himself.

"A birthday cake," he muttered. "I wonder whose birthday it was? Surely not her own."

"Oh, no," Wilma said quickly. "Jeri Lynn was a Gemini. She told me one day when I saw her reading an astrology book."

"Gemini?"

"The twins, and that's in June. This is only February."

"Then it must have been for a friend—a very special friend."

Wilma smiled knowingly. "If you're thinking of the

greeting, that doesn't mean anything. Jeri Lynn called everybody 'darling.' She even called me 'darling' until I told her what I thought of it!"

But Osgood wasn't thinking of the greeting. The Jeri Lynns he'd met—purely in the line of duty, of course—weren't much for giving anything to anyone unless they really rated in one way or another. It seemed peculiar that the intended recipient of that cake hadn't shown up at least to pay respects to that body in the morgue. It was more than twenty-four hours since she'd gone there, and the only nibble so far was from the agent he'd dug out of that phone book, an agent who didn't even know the kid's right name and hadn't seen her in over six months.

"Do you know," he said, because it seemed very natural to talk to this woman who was supposed to be crazy, "that after twenty-four hours no one has appeared to make arrangements for Miss Lynn's funeral?"

Wilma seemed unimpressed. "There may be a very good reason," she suggested.

"What do you mean?"

"Well, I couldn't help noticing that most of Miss Lynn's friends were of the opposite sex. They probably wish to avoid the publicity."

She didn't say what kind of publicity, and Osgood didn't ask. He didn't have to ask. "That may be," he admitted, "but it still seems that there should be someone, a friend, a relative somewhere. She must have had some family."

John Peter Osgood was thinking aloud, and he'd forgotten all about Mr. Sergeant, the insurance man. But Wilma hadn't. He could actually hear her suck in her breath, and then a very sudden cold wave set in. It was as if all this time she had been sitting there waiting for him to say the wrong thing, and now that he had said it, her guard went up like a Congressman in front of a television camera.

"But surely you must know where to find her family,"

she said. "Doesn't her insurance policy name a benefici-
ary?"

Osgood was beginning to think that Wilma Rathjen
should be the investigator of this twosome. "That's not in
my department," he said quickly.

"Really? I see no reason why that information should
be withheld from you. What company do you represent?"

"Oh, it's just a small outfit— Well, thank you for your
help, Miss Rathjen. I don't want to take up any more of
your time—"

"But I have plenty of time, Sergeant."

It wasn't a slip of the tongue. At the beginning Wilma
might have thought he was an insurance man, at the very
beginning. But not for long. Sergeant, lieutenant, captain—
she had the man identified at last. Who but a policeman
would ask such questions? Who but a policeman would
ferret out the information that she worked at a bakery
and had sold Jeri Lynn's cake? Curtis had said the police
wouldn't bother her, but he was wrong. And worst of all,
they had come with tricks and lies because Wilma Rathjen
wasn't to be trusted. Wilma Rathjen wasn't quite right!

Tricks and lies. For a moment Wilma's anger was
stronger than her fear. If only this police sergeant had
come to her openly, as he must have come to the other
tenants, then she might have told him of such interesting
matters as the unreasonable grief of the nurse in the north
front unit, or the mystery of the midnight prowlers. But
now she was forewarned. Now she knew better than to
toss out truth like pennies to beggars. And she was right.
Because this was no insurance man, the time of Jeri Lynn's
death wasn't important—only the means.

From the doorway, and Wilma had no recollection of
when he had left the wing chair, the man who called himself Mr. Sergeant was stammering a hurried good-by. "I
really must be going," he said. "Thank you for your trouble, Miss Rathjen."

Trouble! The instant he was gone Wilma ran across the room and bolted the door. Trouble! Oh, God!

John Peter Osgood left Wilma's apartment a far more confused man than when he arrived. She'd given a perfectly reasonable explanation for that confounded cake, but it was the woman herself that confused him. He'd seen all kinds in nineteen years. He'd dealt with insane killers who seemed more rational than their analysts, and with everything from stark madness to simple senility; but Wilma Rathjen was different from these. And yet, not so different from a lot of people he'd seen around lately. If they started locking up everybody who was scared, as Curtis Rathjen had done with his sister, there probably wouldn't be many people left to pay taxes.

At the foot of the stairs he stopped and let his eyes wander over the courtyard. The blonde Frenchy had been so concerned about was out in the drying-yard hanging up her lingerie, and Frenchy would have enjoyed the view immensely since what she had on was even skimpier than what she was putting on the line. Up at the front of the court the old man in overalls clipped away at the hedges, and out on the narrow strip of grass that separated the buildings a young Adonis in bright-yellow swim trunks was taking a sun bath he didn't need. Browned and muscular, with the black curly hair crawling down the nape of his neck, he looked like a cover boy for some bobbysoxers' fan magazine. With only one of the tenants still unaccounted for, there wasn't much doubt of his identity.

Osgood strolled over and stared down at the youth with distaste in his narrow eyes. He could remember when a healthy specimen like this one was supposed to work for a living; but then Osgood was getting old. When the kid raised his head to see what grew up from the big feet planted alongside his nose, the distaste was returned with interest.

"Hello, copper," he said. "What brings you here?"

"Tony Carmen?" Osgood asked.

"That's right. How did you know?"

"A little chick told me. I've been wanting to have a talk with you."

The kid—he didn't look much over twenty—rolled over on his side and slapped the grass with one hand. "Come on into my private office and have a seat," he invited. "And stop looking like a deacon. What is it I'm supposed to know that you wish you knew?"

John Peter Osgood wasn't a man who expected a red carpet to roll out at his feet every time he met anyone, but smart young punks like Tony Carmen got under his skin. And he didn't feel like sitting down on the grass. He liked it up high.

"Not what you're supposed to know," he corrected, "but who you're supposed to have known."

"Jeri Lynn?"

"Who else? I understand she was a good friend of yours."

"Well, what do you know! And I always thought she couldn't see me with binoculars!"

Tony flashed a big smile that was downright dazzling against all that sun tan, but his heart wasn't in it. It must be tough, Osgood reckoned, for a lady-killer to make such an admission about any woman—even a headline corpse.

"Don't tell me the lady was able to resist your charms," he taunted, and Tony swallowed the bait whole.

"That little bitch! The only things that charmed her were the tinkle of silver and the rustle of folding money! What's this all about anyway? Why don't you let the girl rest in peace?"

"In potter's field?"

"What difference does it make? She'll never know." It was a little late for Tony to feign indifference. Something was burning, and from where Osgood stood it smelled like a torch. Then the boy arched one black eyebrow and managed a twisted grin. "Of course," he added, "you might hock her mink and give her a real send-off."

"Maybe the guy who gave it to her wants it back," Osgood said.

"Why don't you ask him?"

"I would if I knew his name."

This was the time for Tony Carmen to get a load off his chest and start naming names; but either he didn't know any names or was just being stubborn, because all the answer Osgood got for his trouble was a penetrating stare. Any moment now and the kid was going to start asking a few questions of his own. If Jeri Lynn was just another bathroom casualty, why all the nosing around? Until Frenchy came back, Osgood couldn't answer that one even to suit himself, but Tony Carmen's evaluation of the dead girl matched up pretty well with what Osgood suspected and what the woman on the roof had implied in a more genteel manner. All of it made that birthday cake seem all the more interesting, and he was just about to ask Tony the color of his raincoat when a cab pulled up to the curb and a young soldier stepped out.

He was a nice-looking kid, not handsome but just about the way any proud father would like his son to look. He had a high-school boy's face and a row of ribbons on his chest that hadn't come from any R.O.T.C. unit, and he seemed to know exactly where he was going. After paying off the driver, he studied the row of numbers posted on the corner of Ann Jenner's unit and then, bag in hand, sauntered down the center walk as if he owned the place.

"New boy," Tony murmured. "Those gals behind me play no favorites. Every branch of the service is welcome here. It's sort of a subsidiary USO."

But the soldier didn't stop at the entrance back of Tony's apartment. He squinted at the number and kept right on going until he reached Jeri Lynn's door. There he stopped, pulled a key out of his pants pocket, and proceeded to let himself in. The whole performance was so unexpected Osgood could only stand by with his mouth open.

"Who—" he began, but Tony was already shrugging.

"Don't ask me," he said. "I never saw the guy before."

Osgood and Tony Carmen weren't the only spectators to the new arrival. The old man with the hedge clippers dropped his work and came trotting across the courtyard, but at the sight of Osgood he pulled up short to demand what was going on and what kind of a policeman was he to stand by while a stranger broke into one of the apartments? Of course the soldier hadn't broken into anything. He had a key, and why he had a key was something Osgood intended to find out as soon as he brushed aside the one-man vigilante committee.

The door was closed again by the time he reached it, but so was Osgood's fist. On about the fourth knuckle-bruising attempt the door swung open, and he found himself facing a slender kid with fire in both eyes.

"Take it easy, Mac," the soldier said. "We might want to use this door again."

It looked as if the kid had been making himself right at home. His cap was off, his tie was loosened, and a couple of drawers were pulled open on the desk. Osgood couldn't see much of the room with the doorway blocked, but he did catch the canvas bag that had been dropped just inside the door. It had a name stenciled on the side: Blade, Phillip.

"Do you know who's apartment you're in?" he asked, and the kid's anger gave way to a timid grin.

"You must be the landlord," he said.

"Wrong guess. I'm a policeman."

"A policeman! Christ, does this place have a house dick now? I should have been warned!"

The situation didn't seem particularly amusing, but Osgood had to wait until the kid finished a weak laugh at his own private joke. Then he asked if he knew Jeri Lynn, and the soldier's answer made an awful hole in the conversation.

"Sure, I know her," he said, "and I've been waiting fourteen months for the chance to know her better. But I know her as Mrs. Phillip Blade."

CHAPTER SEVEN

Just when about everybody but John Peter Osgood was ready to forget about Jeri Lynn, along came a good-looking soldier with a row of ribbons on his chest and a load of grief in store that was going to stir up the excitement all over again. The soldier didn't seem to fit in the picture at all. Standing there on the cement porch with a foolish expression on his face, Osgood was acutely aware of that fact. The portrait of the dead girl that he'd been piecing together with scraps of observation, hearsay, and experience didn't have room for a bridegroom in it, particularly not a slim-hipped kid with a high-school boy's face and a Pfc.'s pay. At least, that's how the situation struck him when the soldier made his surprise announcement, and it must have hit Tony Carmen the same way.

"Holy Jupiter!" Tony gasped at his shoulder. "There really is one born every minute!"

It was no way to go about wiping off the soldier's fading grin, and without it he didn't look so boyish. Without it he looked like a man who had earned all those ribbons the hard way. "What do you mean by a crack like that?" he demanded, but Tony never got the chance to answer.

"He don't mean a damn thing!" Wallace Timm snapped. "He just has to flap his dirty mouth because a nice girl like your wife wouldn't have anything to do with him!"

It was a surprising opinion to come from any quarter, Osgood thought, and particularly from an old man with no personal interest in the matter; but Timm probably reckoned that the kid had enough grief coming to him without being subjected to a sidewalk analysis of his dead wife's character. If so, Osgood could concur. He wasn't crazy about his job at any time, but a deal like this made him wish he'd never let them hang that badge on his chest nineteen years ago, even if it was steady work and he did have a score to even. Blade started asking questions, and he parried them as long as he could, while he tried to think of a painless method for sticking a knife in a man's heart. He heard about the marriage that had taken place on Blade's last week-end pass before sailing overseas, and of how she'd kept the marriage a secret because of her career. He heard quite a bit of what a man thinks about having an audience at the intended reunion with his wife.

"Did you just get in?" Osgood asked.

The soldier was red up to his ears by this time. He just didn't seem to be a very patient man.

"What does it look like?" he said. "I haven't seen my wife in a long time, officer, so if you don't mind—"

"Then I guess you haven't seen the papers either."

It was no use. Delaying the operation wouldn't make that knife hurt any less. So Osgood invited Phillip Blade out to the sedan Frenchy had just rolled up to the curb, and the three of them had a long talk on the way to the morgue.

"If you ask me, the kid's getting off easy," Frenchy said later. "What he doesn't know about his wife won't hurt him."

It was quite a bit later. It was after the morgue and the questioning at headquarters. It was after they'd turned the kid over to the none too tender mercies of the newsmen who'd picked up the scent of a story that was going to go over big with the motherly readers of the late editions. A young, clean-cut American hero had come home from fourteen months' overseas duty only to find his beautiful wife dead. But that wasn't all of Phillip Blade's sad story. The rest of it came out when he explained about Jeri's lack of mourners.

"She didn't have any folks," he said, "just like me. My old man skipped when I was a baby, and my mother died when I was ten years old. With Jeri it was the same deal. That was something we had in common."

"Then I take it you weren't school-day sweethearts," Frenchy remarked.

Blade looked nervous. After all the fight he'd shown at the bungalow, Osgood had been afraid of how he might take the bad news. But the kid had his emotions under control. He was just jumpy and nervous.

"If it's anybody's business, we met at a bar," he said.

"How long before you were married?"

"A couple of weeks. What's this all about, anyway? Why all the questions? Didn't you say Jeri's death was an accident?"

"Sure," Frenchy muttered, "that's what we said."

Osgood knew from Frenchy's attitude that he must have picked up something interesting on that excursion to Elaine's, and as soon as the soldier was packed off with his private grief, the whole story came out. There was no place quite like a beauty parlor for digging up dirt, and Frenchy needed a wheelbarrow for all he'd gathered on Jeri Lynn.

"The story on our bathroom casualty is that she'd been angling for a fat bank roll and was just about set to reel it in," Frenchy reported. Then he paused to reflect on his own words. "Unless," he added, "Phillip Blade is coming into a fortune."

In view of what Blade had been telling them, there wasn't much chance of that unless his father turned up as another Daddy Warbucks. "What about Tuesday afternoon?" Osgood reminded, but Frenchy was more interested in that wheelbarrow.

"I'm working up to that," he said, studying his fingernails. They were beautiful fingernails, freshly manicured. "But I want you to get the picture just as I got it from Elaine. It seems that Jeri was a long-time customer. She'd been getting her overhaul jobs from Elaine ever since she worked up the street at La Rene's Place."

Frenchy buffed his nails on a tweed lapel and watched Osgood's eyebrows grow together. "I thought that would interest you," he added. "Of course, La Rene's supposed to have reformed since we closed her last couple of dives, but you know how far that goes. But don't get me wrong. According to Elaine, Jeri was a legitimate entertainer, a dancer in the floor show. She seemed to be doing pretty well, too, and then about six months ago she quit the job cold. Elaine thinks that must have been when she met the bank roll and decided that belly dancing wasn't a proper occupation for a girl out to snag a wealthy husband."

"Wait a minute," Osgood objected. "She already had a husband."

It was just as well he didn't have to hear the lecture that went with the disdainful expression on Frenchy's face. Acquainting John Peter Osgood with the facts of life was Frenchy's pet hobby, but even an overaged Boy Scout should appreciate the fact that a girl trying to get on in the world wouldn't hesitate to discard a bad investment such as Phillip Blade.

"She couldn't buy mink with allotment checks," he pointed out, which only went to prove that Frenchy Bartel kept his eyes open, too.

But the most important part of his story was missing. Elaine didn't know the identity of that alleged bank roll—didn't know or wouldn't tell. She only knew that Jeri had been playing for it a long time, and had come in Tuesday afternoon all excited about a big date that was going to change her whole life.

"She even promised an inflation-sized tip if Elaine would

do an extra-special job," Frenchy related, "on the cuff, understand, since she was pretty hard up for cash since quitting her job. Seeing that her livelihood depended on looking beautiful, Elaine went for it, and now she's the unhappiest woman in town. Jeri had the works—facial, manicure, and a brand-new hair-do. All dry and combed out, by the way."

That was the information Frenchy had gone after, but it came as an anticlimax. That big date was a lot more interesting because it had never come off—or maybe it had in a way Jeri Lynn hadn't planned. It was another part of what had disturbed Osgood about that death apartment. The dinner gown on the bed, the obvious preparation for a big night with someone, and then almost two days before the body was discovered. It seemed that if a man was stood up that long he would at least make an inquiry. Unless maybe he knew what was wrong.

So they put their heads together and added an interview with Elaine to a visit with Wilma Rathjen, tossed in the appearance of an unexpected husband, and topped the whole thing off with a missing birthday cake. There were explanations for the hair dryer—an accidental shove, a careless elbow—but they sounded pretty unconvincing alongside all the other developments.

"A tall young man in a tan raincoat," Osgood murmured. "I wonder if the Rathjen woman knows what she's talking about."

It didn't matter too much. With a description like that the task of tracking down Jeri Lynn's mysterious bank roll could turn into a lifetime occupation. A better way seemed to be to start at the beginning, or at least as near the beginning as anyone seemed to know.

The day was far gone when Osgood left headquarters and drove off in his own battered sedan. There was no sunset. The ball of fire in the west just dropped into the ocean, and then the fog rolled in like a cloud of steam. For most people the day was over. Phillip Blade was all fixed up with accommodations in one of the more plush hotels (courtesy of a circulation-minded daily), Frenchy Bartel had rushed off to get a shave before picking up the date he'd made during his travels, and Jeri Lynn, with all her dates behind her, still had a slab for the night in the county morgue. Everybody was all fixed up, including Osgood, who could go home and watch television as soon as he picked up a loaf of wheat-germ bread.

Although there were hundreds of bakeries in the city, only one of them was located across the parking lot from La Rene's Place, and Osgood had never learned to check his curiosity at the desk when he went home. It was late dusk by the time he finished his chore and headed across the lot. The floodlights had come on, and all the painted faces that worried Wilma so much were smiling as he passed by. Osgood was not enticed. To his cynical eyes one painted face was like every other painted face. There had been one a long time ago—but it was crazy to even think of that now. A woman would have to be a fool to marry a man and an invalid.

But one item in Frenchy's report did give the faces on the billboard a special significance. Jeri Lynn had been an entertainer at La Rene's. It could have been six months or six years ago, La Rene would remember. La Rene Flavin never forgot a face, a friend, or an enemy.

On the outside the building was a blaze of light, but on the inside it looked as if somebody had forgotten to pay the electric bill. The dining-room wasn't open yet, and it would have taken a seeing-eye dog to find it; but the bar was ringed with a scattering of cocktail-hour customers as well as a few holdovers from lunch or even breakfast. There was nothing formal about the atmosphere at La Rene's. Overalls, slacks, dinner clothes—any attire at all was acceptable as long as it had pockets. When the guided tours took the folks from Cedar Rapids to see the Holly-wood sights, they never stopped or even drove past La Rene's Place; but La Rene was more of a sight than any-thing they would see. La Rene was the battered remains of an old-time show girl with a scrapbook full of memo-ries, a bankbook full of souvenirs, and enough practical knowledge to make a schoolboy of Bernard Baruch. Being a realist, she didn't mind an occasional padlock during a hot election—the girls needed a rest now and then anyway; and if an ax in a dice table made a good picture in the *Morning Blurb*, it only meant that twice as many suckers would be asking where she was moving to next. The law held no terrors for La Rene—particularly not when it came in the person of John Peter Osgood with a loaf of bread under his arm.

"Hello, Happy," she called out from behind the bar. "Who died?"

From behind the bar you couldn't see how generously La Rene filled out the black gabardine slacks that were a part of her daytime costume. Black slacks, white blouse, and sometimes a ruffled apron if a special banquet needed kitchen supervision; but before the heavy trade got under way she'd disappear for a time and come back wearing enough sequins to outfit the chorus of a Technicolor movie. Osgood knew this because he'd done enough night duty to be familiar with La Rene's routine, and since his visits were usually official, she broke off the liquor inven-tory she'd been taking and joined him at the uncrowded end of the bar.

"All right, out with it," she said. "What's your grief to-day, Sergeant?"

"Does it have to be grief?" Osgood answered. "Maybe I just dropped in for a beer."

"Not with that loaf of bread under your arm. Mamma might smell your breath when you get home."

La Rene was only kidding—he could tell by the way

she flashed her bridgework—but she shouldn't have talked that way to a man with a suppressed desire to shove a fist through her face. But then La Rene didn't know about that. Osgood usually managed to keep his blood pressure where it didn't show.

"You had a girl working here some time back," he began.

"I've had a lot of girls working here."

"This one had her picture in the papers last night."

La Rene's eyes remembered before her tongue. "You must mean Jeri Lynn."

"Then you remember her."

"Sure, I remember her. She was a cute kid. Not much of a dancer, but she had what the customers want to see. You know, decorative."

Decorative seemed like a good word for Jeri Lynn. She would have looked real decorative on the billboards outside.

"Why did she quit?" Osgood asked, and La Rene responded with a burst of laughter that rocked the glasses on the bar.

"Quit? Hell, Sergeant, that little tart didn't quit! I tied a can to her tail!"

It was a peculiar thing about character witnesses. A dozen upright citizens could have sworn affidavits that Jeri Lynn was a tramp, and Osgood might have retained a reasonable doubt; but when a woman like La Rene Flavin placed a name on anyone it had to fit. La Rene had no interest in nonprofit malice and no need of an outlet for the larceny in her soul. So far as Osgood was concerned, the portrait of the dead girl was now complete. What was missing was the other half of an alleged twosome that might well have had its meeting under this very roof.

"So you fired her," he mused. "Any particular reason?"

"A damn particular reason. I didn't like the play she

was making for my husband."

Ask this woman a question and you got an answer! The swift surprise on Osgood's face had a *double-entendre* that brought back La Rene's laughter. "Oh, I know that Matt's no prize," she added, "but I still have my pride. Nobody takes that lush away from me, especially when the big attraction is his share of the community property. I've earned every cent of that property myself, and I don't feel generous."

La Rene wasn't exaggerating her devaluation of Matt Flavin. Now that his eyes were getting used to the darkness, Osgood had no trouble recognizing the big red-faced man in a loud sport jacket who was holding down one of the far stools. Matt Flavin held the dubious rank of stage director for La Rene's floor shows, although his only directorial skill seemed to lie in the art of guiding a steady flow of liquor to his lips. Once in a while La Rene shipped him off for a cure that never lasted, but most of the time he stumbled about in a state of happy oblivion. Matt might have been a dashing dandy thirty years ago. Today he was just an oversized cosigner on La Rene's bank account, and, although that might have been enough for a girl like Jeri Lynn, it was hard to picture him looking like a tall young man in a tan raincoat or any other garb.

"What about a fellow named Tony Carmen?" Osgood asked. "Know him?"

"I should," La Rene answered. "He's been trying to convince me he's a trumpet player ever since I opened this place."

"Ever see him come in with Jeri Lynn?"

The trouble with asking so many questions of La Rene Flavin was that she usually finished a couple of jumps ahead. By this time she was frowning like a C.P.A. poring over a tax form, and under that bleached and curly head the wheels were spinning fast.

"Sure," she said. "A year or so ago Tony tried to sell me

an act with the two of them. I took Jeri—she didn't play a trumpet. Now what the hell's this all about, Sergeant? I thought Jeri's death was accidental."

"Nobody said it wasn't."

"Nobody but you and your God-damn long nose! You know how it looks to me? It looks to me like you've been checking up on the kid and decided that maybe it's true what they say about only the good dying young. Am I right?"

La Rene had Osgood cold. Quick comebacks weren't his specialty, and he was still groping for an answer when Matt Flavin reached the bottom of his glass and called for another refill. Without the lull in the conversation he might have got away with it, but La Rene heard him and countermanded the order in the voice of a dock foreman. "One more drink and you'll be out so cold even the cancan number won't open your eyes!" she yelled, and Matt obediently backed away from the bar and melted into the shadows.

Around Matt all was darkness; but around Osgood a bright light had begun to show.

"Well?" La Rene demanded, and Osgood remembered that he still had a question to answer or dodge.

"For the sake of argument, let's say that you are right," he said. "Being a woman of many contacts, you must know all the local gossip. Can you think of anyone with a real good reason for wanting Jeri Lynn dead?"

It was a cards-on-the-table question, and he got a cards-on-the-table reply.

"Of course I can," she said. "Her husband."

La Rene was a spoilsport. Just when Osgood was getting excited about that inadvertent inspiration she'd given him, the woman had to remind him of an unpleasant truth. If all these stories about his wife were true, Phillip Blade certainly did have a motive for murder. No one had bothered to verify the kid's story that he was just getting home. Why should they? His wife had just died in a tragic bathroom accident. He was an object of pity not suspicion.

But if there was anything in La Rene's suggestion, it would take a lot more than a missing birthday cake and some beauty-parlor gossip to make a case. The old stucco bungalow court was only a few blocks away, and that last drink Matt didn't get reminded Osgood of a bothersome detail that would have to be cleared up before anyone could make murder out of a stupid accident. Nobody was going to sit still while someone tossed a live appliance in the bath water, but out on the drainboard of Jeri Lynn's sink was a bottle of Scotch that could have held a lot of oblivion. It seemed a peculiar place to keep the liquor unless she was an awfully sloppy housekeeper, and it was just possible that a man who knew what he was looking for might scour up a pair of glasses in a similar state of untidiness.

At this hour the center walk was crossed by bars of light and the whole courtyard smelled of fried food and fresh coffee. Tony Carmen must have been playing records because the trumpet-playing coming from his apartment didn't match La Rene's implied appraisal, and the girls next door were retaliating with something written for a bunch of toe dancers with a high vitamin content. In all that homey bedlam nobody was going to notice one policeman coming back to that apartment that was beginning to seem like a home away from home.

It looked so much shabbier under artificial light. Shabbier and smaller and even more cluttered than Osgood remembered. The unpaid bills were stacked on the desk top, and those two drawers were still standing open; but Blade hadn't been alone in the place more than a couple of minutes, so he couldn't have done too much damage. Leaving a blaze of lights behind him, Osgood went straight to the kitchen where the bottle of Scotch still stood on the drainboard. The sink held only a half a cup of cold coffee with a couple of floating cigarette butts and an empty ice-cube tray, but Osgood wasn't discouraged. A pantry-sized kitchen was no place to entertain anyway.

It was about five minutes and three rooms later that he finally found what he was looking for. It was rolled halfway under the divan in the living-room, and it did seem a rather peculiar place to leave the glassware.

Osgood was beginning to love Matt Flavin. With the protective aid of his handkerchief, he retrieved the glass and sniffed at the few drops of amber liquid still remaining at the bottom. Not being a drinking man, he couldn't identify all the ingredients, but it wasn't lemonade. There was no indication of a party or even a second imbiber, but it was obvious that in the not-too-distant past someone had occupied the divan, polished off a drink, and then let the glass slip to the floor. It might have been Jeri, it might not, but because the hunch had paid off so far he wrapped the handkerchief around the glass and stuffed the roll into his jacket pocket. After that he went back to the bathroom for one last look around.

He wanted to fix the picture in his mind. The tub was in the far corner from the door. The ledge where the hair dryer stood was opposite the faucets, and that meant Jeri would have had her back to the dryer as she sat facing the door. There was no possibility of an unseen intruder, which bore out his idea that the girl must have been un-conscious or on awfully good terms with any possible killer. He looked inside the medicine chest for anything that might have assisted a lapse of consciousness, but Jeri Lynn must have been a healthy girl. Aside from a roll of adhesive tape and a bottle of mouthwash there was noth-ing in the medicinal line at all.

And yet there were many ways to turn this accident into murder—too many ways in an apartment that had been unlocked and in a court filled with so many individualists concerned only with their own problems. It did seem that at least one of them might have had some idea of who Jeri Lynn's big date could be—

Osgood got no further with his tubside reflections. Aside from the distant thumping of the music in the next apartment, all was quiet and pensive until the scream came. It was a blood-chilling scream that split the night and left it quivering, and it was followed by an ear-tingling ultimatum.

"Don't you move! Don't you come toward me! One step and I'll cut you to ribbons!"

CHAPTER EIGHT

Wilma's day had been one of mounting apprehension. The anxiety of the morning was only accelerated by Osgood's visit, for if the police were still investigating Jeri Lynn's death, all her fears were well founded. From her wide front window—cranked open to catch every possible word—she witnessed the arrival of the soldier and heard enough of that doorstep conversation to realize that the sergeant was greatly agitated about something. She would have liked to have ventured downstairs to share in the courtyard gossip that commenced with the departure of the soldier and the police; but Wilma knew she wasn't welcome in the courtyard. It wasn't only that she was the landlord's sister and therefore an object of suspicion. She was Wilma Rathjen, a nosy old maid who spied on tenants and made up tales.

But surely this was no fabricated problem. Paired with the puzzle of last night's prowlers, it began to assume gigantic proportions. She decided to risk the party line and call Curtis.

It wasn't easy getting past Curtis's secretary. It was even less easy getting past Curtis.

"I can't speak freely," she confided, in a tense, frightened voice, "but I have something of vital importance to discuss with you. It concerns J.L."

"It concerns *what?*" Curtis echoed.

"J.L. You know, the party we were discussing last night."

Behind the pause on the opposite end of the wire came a low groan. "Not that again!" he protested.

"Again? I've no idea what you're talking about!"

"I can believe that! What's more, I doubt if you have any idea what you're talking about. Have you been listening to the radio again?"

Wilma held the telephone at arm's length and stared helplessly at the offending object. Curtis wouldn't listen! He wouldn't listen, and he wouldn't come because he thought she was imagining things again! And she couldn't go to him. His office was across town—she was never quite sure where—and even if she could find it he would be angry with her for barging in among his associates. Not that he would say anything, but she could tell. At times Wilma actually felt psychic.

"Why don't you take a hot bath and lie down for a while?" Curtis suggested. "And don't call me back. I'm busy."

The click of the receiver was like a little knife cutting her off from her last hope of comfort. Now she was even more alone than before the call, and a swarm of worries began to gather like hornets about her head. With no one to drive them off, fancy soon became fact, and fact was a frightful thing. Jeri Lynn had been murdered, and the police were watching her—that's all she could possibly think. At least she'd kept the sergeant out of the kitchen and away from the cake. She ran into the kitchen and hid the huge cake box far back on the highest cupboard shelf. It was all she could think to do at the moment.

"Take a hot bath and lie down for a while."

Curtis's words came back to mind, and Wilma shuddered. At such times even the most innocent words could take on an ominous significance. Jeri Lynn had taken a hot bath and died. How strange that Curtis should suggest such a thing. But Curtis always had been thoughtless. Wilma began to remember things that should have been forgotten, old things warped and twisted with time. She remembered the way Curtis used to play in the fields while she kept watch beside Mamma's bed. Had he ever given up one hour of child's play to relieve her of the vigil? Had he ever thought then to watch for the evil that waited in the darkness?

One vigil was like another. Because she had watched for so many years, Wilma watched again. She drew a chair close to the window and watched the center walk for whatever strange terror came next. But for a long time there was nothing but the coming and going of the tenants, the theatricals with their free and easy manners, the young man in bathing trunks with such flagrant pride in his nakedness, and old Wallace Timm puttering about the hedges and grumbling about all the work he had to do. And so the day passed, and all the time the evil seemed to be moving closer.

Wilma didn't realize it was so late until she saw Ruby Lennox swagger off into the dusk, and it was only because of Alice that she left the window then. Alice watched nothing but the refrigerator door, and when it didn't open on schedule, she issued a noisy protest. From the kitchen Wilma could watch nothing but the tall hulk of the incinerator in the small yard behind the garages—but she could hear, and what she heard, as she stood at the work table slicing liver for the cat, was a sound on the stairs that made her pulse quicken.

Wilma didn't like uninvited guests, particularly not when they came as stealthily as a thief. Ears less accustomed to listening might not have heard the footsteps at all, but the stairway creaked, and Wilma drew in her breath. It might be Curtis. Perhaps he'd relented and come to answer her call after all, but Curtis wouldn't steal so quietly or take so long. She waited a few seconds and then, still clutching the knife she'd been using to slice the liver, slipped quietly through the shuttered doorway and opened the outer door. The roof deck was lost in the late darkness, but no sooner had Wilma peered down into the courtyard than she forgot about the creaking stairs.

The light was burning in Jeri Lynn's bathroom again. For one awful moment Wilma was afraid to look. The devil himself only knew what she might see this time! But it was only the man who called himself Mr. Sergeant who moved into view and stood looking down into the tub. Only! What could the man be looking for to come again and again? Fascinated, Wilma watched and pondered the puzzle while the worry gnawed like hunger at her mind, and then, from the very corner of her eye she caught a glimpse of something that was beyond all endurance. Not six feet distant a tall man-shadow was leaning against the roof-deck railing pointing a weapon at the bright window below!

Wilma had no weapon but a kitchen knife, but she had the scream of a banshee—

It took Osgood about ten seconds to determine where the scream had come from and not much longer to take the garage stairs at a dead run. What he found above was somewhat anticlimactic to one expecting nothing less than human gore. Wilma had scurried to safety behind a bolted screen door and was peering out like a terrified animal in a cage; and her visitor, clearly visible under a sudden flood of an outdoor light, looked more like a man caught in public without his pants than the instigator of such fright. His weapon was a flash camera and his voice a startled squeak.

"Take it easy, lady," he was pleading. "I'm not Jack the Ripper!"

Most of the news cameramen in the city were familiar to Osgood, but this was a man he'd never seen before. There wasn't much of him to see. He wasn't much huskier than that woman behind the screen door, and if it hadn't been for that professional camera he was holding up where his chest should have been, Osgood might have mistaken him for one of Tony Carmen's equestrian friends.

"What are you doing up here?" he demanded, and the little man acquired a foolish grin.

"Just getting camera angles," he said. "From up here you can get the whole layout."

"Of what?"

"I don't know yet, Sergeant. Maybe you can tell me." The grin was growing into a full-fledged smile because this Peeping Tom with the flash camera wasn't kidding about the view. How long he might have been on the roof was something Osgood didn't know, but long enough, obviously, to work up a curiosity about all those lights in the dead girl's apartment. The fact that he knew Osgood's rating seemed to indicate that he recognized to whom he was talking even if Osgood didn't recognize him.

"Who sent you out here?" Osgood snapped.

"Nobody. I came on my own. I sort of free-lance."

"Well, suppose you free-lance yourself off these premises before you get arrested for trespassing."

Being a bright lad, the intruder was putting Osgood's suggestion to good use when the screen door burst open on a sight that would have held anyone spellbound. With the law on her side Wilma seemed to lose her fear, and she was a rather terrible sight as she charged out on the roof waving the knife that was still clutched in one hand.

"Don't let him get away!" she cried. "Smash his camera!"

Osgood wasn't sure who the command was for, because she seemed intent on carrying it out herself. A little fast footwork and a basketball reach were all that saved the object, and by this time the little man was doing some vocalizing of his own. "What's the matter with this crazy dame?" he yelled. "First she wants to knife me, now she wants to smash my camera! What kind of a nut is she?"

"Shut up!" Osgood snapped.

It was one of the few times in his life that John Peter Osgood issued an order and had it instantly obeyed. The man with the camera shut up, Wilma shut up, and down in the courtyard where her first scream had summoned a ring of faces that peered upward like spellbound spectators at a trapeze act, everybody shut up. Crazy dame—nut— these were colloquialisms Wilma Rathjen must surely understand. He looked to see how she was reacting to them, and she backed slowly toward the door.

"He took a picture," she protested weakly. "I saw him take a picture."

"Never mind, Miss Rathjen. I'll see that he doesn't take any more."

Osgood meant what he said, but he reckoned without the camera bug. "Rathjen—" the man murmured. "Say, does this dump belong to Curtis Rathjen?"

"You leave my brother out of this!" Wilma cried.

"Your brother!"

"Yes, my brother! He's a very important man, and he doesn't want reporters hanging around this property! He doesn't want policemen hanging around either, so get out! Both of you get out!"

Osgood could see what was happening, but he couldn't stop it in time. Hysterics came with gestures, and with a knife in her hand Wilma had begun to look like a fugitive from a strait jacket. It was a dead heat between her cry and the flash of the camera.

"You crazy fool!" Osgood bawled. "Rathjen will have your scalp if that picture is printed!"

But he was shouting to himself. By this time the little man with the camera was racing downstairs looking as happy as if he'd just caught a college president coming out of a Communist rally, and Wilma had either disintegrated or fled inside the apartment. It made a nice ending to the day, Osgood thought, and hell to pay tomorrow if Curtis Rathjen found that unposed portrait on the front page.

Osgood had a habit of worrying about the wrong things.

CHAPTER NINE

Wilma worried, too, but her dread wasn't long in materializing. It came early the next morning shortly after she'd called the supervisor to say she was too sick to come to work. She wasn't really sick, not bodily at any rate, but she didn't dare leave her apartment now that some terrible doom was closing in about the courtyard like the devil's own embrace. She'd no more than completed the call before Curtis telephoned to suggest the same thing. From the sound of his voice, Curtis wasn't feeling well either.

"Sit tight and don't leave the apartment," he ordered. "I'm coming right over. And don't talk to anyone!"

At such an early hour there was no one about for Wilma to talk to except Alice, but the very fact that Curtis stressed the point gave Wilma a clue to his anxiety. She must have talked to someone and said too much. But to whom? The only person she had really talked to was the policeman who called himself Mr. Sergeant, and she certainly hadn't said anything wrong to him! Wilma didn't have long to wait for the denouement of her puzzle. Within half an hour Curtis was at her door, red-faced and furious.

"Well," he demanded, "what have you got to say for yourself this time?"

He didn't usually bark at her that way. The hurt flooded Wilma's eyes so that she hardly noticed the wide Manila envelope he clutched in one tight hand; but she noticed soon enough when he ripped open the flap and handed her the contents. It was that terrible picture the man with the camera had taken last night. It was even worse than Wilma thought. She looked like a madwoman charging at the camera with a knife upraised like a cavalry saber.

"Where did you get this?" she gasped.

"By special messenger," Curtis said. "And there was a note with it, a subtle suggestion that I might like to purchase the negative rather than have it fall into the hands of certain people. Hang it all, Wil', you know that the minute a man tries to get anywhere in his community there's always somebody trying to drag him down. I've been suggested as a candidate for City Council. Suppose that I decided to make the race and my opponent came up with this!"

Curtis didn't have to go into detail. What he was saying was that a public figure couldn't afford to have a sister who went about brandishing knives at people. Wilma understood.

"But who would do such a thing?" she said weakly. "Who would send you that picture and the letter?"

"The man who took the picture, I suppose," Curtis snapped. "Who was he? What was he doing here?"

Wilma couldn't very well answer what she didn't know.

"I never saw him before last night," she said. "He came up on my sun deck and started taking pictures. I didn't want him here so I tried to drive him off."

"With a knife?"

"I didn't even know that I had the knife. I'd been slicing liver for Alice, and then I heard the noise and saw the lights—" Wilma began to rub her temples with her finger tips. It was so hard to remember with Curtis looking at her in such a way. "And then I ran out and told him to leave," she added.

"Is that all you told him? Are you sure you didn't say

that I'd told you to drive off reporters and policemen? It's all in the note, and it doesn't look very nice in black and white!"

An angry Curtis Rathjen was red-faced and bloated like a blowfish, but a dejected Curtis Rathjen was as flabby as a deflated tire. Both emotions were battling for predominance when he crossed the room and dropped down into the big wing chair. Then he seemed to lose his anger and stared up at Wilma with the eyes of an offended little boy.

"I don't know what I'm going to do with you, Wil'." He sighed. "I honestly don't know!"

"It's not my fault!" Wilma cried. "I haven't said anything! I'm not to blame if the police are suspicious!"

"Suspicious?" Lights flickered on in Curtis's tired eyes. "Suspicious of what?"

Wilma stood very still in the center of the living-room, her hands clasped tightly in front of her waist. Her chin lifted just a bit, and the faintest trace of a smile shadowed the corners of her mouth. Of what indeed! For just an instant she seemed to be the keeper of all the secrets in the world. And then she shook her head.

"I don't know," she answered. "I only know that the man who calls himself Mr. Sergeant keeps coming back, and he's a policeman."

Curtis had never heard of Mr. Sergeant. He was too busy to listen before the trouble came, and so now he had to draw out the story sentence by sentence and word by word. "He didn't tell me he was a policeman," Wilma admitted, "but I knew almost from the beginning. Last night was the proof."

"Wait a minute," Curtis broke in. "There was mention in the paper of a Sergeant Osgood who found that soldier yesterday."

"There, you see! I was right! I knew all the time that a girl like Jeri Lynn wouldn't be practical enough to carry insurance!"

Wilma couldn't understand the sudden apprehension in Curtis's eyes. Knowing nothing of Osgood's masquerade, her words were pure gibberish. And then she came out with something that almost knocked him off the chair.

"The first time the sergeant came to see me was to ask about the birthday cake," she said.

"The what?" Curtis sputtered.

"The birthday cake. He wanted to know who claimed Miss Lynn's birthday cake after she was dead. It's store business."

Ordinarily that explanatory afterthought would have satisfied Curtis, but not this time. He wanted to know all about the cake and why the policeman thought it was so important. He was almost as persistent as the sergeant had been, and before she realized what she was doing Wilma had told him about the man in the raincoat. A lie always came easier at the second telling, and truth had a way of becoming what one wanted to believe. By this time Wilma almost believed in the man herself.

"But you explained everything," Curtis remarked when she finished the story. "What brought Osgood back last night?"

"He came to search the apartment again."

"This apartment?"

The mere thought took Wilma's breath. "Of course not! It's Miss Lynn's apartment that he searches. I've stood right here at this window and watched him go from room to room—"

Stopping the way she did only made Wilma's *faux pas* more obvious. That was the trouble with trying to explain things—it was so easy to say too much. The last thing in the world that she wanted was for Curtis to look out that window and realize what kind of view she'd had for that terrible time before the dead girl was found; but Curtis was getting out of the chair and coming toward her with a kind of puzzlement in his eyes. She backed against the blinds as if to cut off the view with her small body.

"I can't imagine what he's looking for," she said quickly. "Can you?"

"Why should I?" Curtis snapped.

"Why, I don't know that you should at all. But then you did know the girl much better than I did. You leased the apartment to her, and you came to collect the rent. At least I hope that's why you came."

Curtis stopped in his tracks. So naked was her implication that the window was forgotten. "What are you driving at?" he demanded, and Wilma almost smiled.

"Don't you think I recognize your car when I see it?"

"My car? What kind of nonsense is this? What have you been telling that policeman?"

"Nothing, Curtis. I've told him nothing at all. That's what you told me to do, wasn't it? To say nothing to the police, or the reporters, or to Katherine."

Wilma watched Curtis wilt before her eyes, and it gave her a strange sense of exultation. He wasn't stupid. He may have guessed her preknowledge of Jeri Lynn's death, but he wouldn't say anything about it now. Curtis was vulnerable, actually vulnerable, and this unexpected revelation was like a doorway to freedom and power. From the corner of her eye she could see what was happening now in the courtyard below, but nothing could dull the edge or triumph in her voice.

"Of course, I wouldn't have told anyway," she added with a thin smile, "because you are my brother and families must stand together in times of trouble. But if you think I've done wrong and should tell the police all I know, well, look down in the courtyard, Curtis. Sergeant Osgood is with us again."

Sergeant Osgood was having a busy morning. He'd made a quick trip to the police lab after that rooftop argument and left a memento in the shape of one highball glass slightly moist inside. After that he'd gone home to worry about what might be on the front page of the morning paper if that fast operator with the camera found a market for his art, and found some comfort when the dawn brought no rage of Rathjen to add to his troubles. What it did bring was a report from the lab that really set the wheels turning. A hunch was a one-man affair, but evidence was something to submit to the coroner and the higher brass. The evidence was scant but provocative. The only fingerprints found on the glass were those of the dead girl, and the contents checked out to be Scotch and water generously laced with a barbiturate. The drug hadn't dissolved as readily in alcohol as it would have in water alone, and there was plenty of evidence that Jeri Lynn had taken a Mickey Finn cocktail before her bath. It didn't seem a very logical action for a girl hurrying to dress for a big date.

Osgood was pondering the situation when Frenchy crawled in and dropped into the nearest chair. Frenchy's eyes had varicose veins, and his disposition had curdled overnight.

"I hate bright sunny mornings," he muttered. "What right has the sun to feel so good when I feel so lousy?"

"The sun went to bed last night," Osgood muttered.

"Don't remind me! That's the last time I try to break down the resistance of a redhead. I never saw a woman drink so much with no effect. She had to take me home!"

Osgood listened with only one ear. Frenchy's romantic escapades constituted the usual morning conversation, and he'd learned to go right ahead with whatever he was doing, in this instance searching his desk for Jeri Lynn's book of personal telephone numbers. But when the redhead in question acquired the identity of a manicurist he'd dated at Elaine's yesterday, Osgood's interest began to stir.

"All in the line of duty, of course," he said, and Frenchy's grin corrugated his nose.

"Maybe not all. I'm a man who likes to be comfortable while he works. But I didn't waste the chance to ask a few more questions about our gorgeous corpse. I had a hunch yesterday that Elaine was holding something back. According to Red, she has her own idea who Jeri's boy friend was but she's not talking for personal reasons."

"Such as?"

"Well, such as losing her lease maybe. And who do you think her landlord is? Curtis Rathjen!"

Frenchy looked as happy as a contestant who's just answered the jackpot question. Osgood began to fear for his mental health.

"Oh, fine," he said, "that's all we need! Can't you find anyone else to link with Jeri Lynn's past? How about the mayor or a couple of councilmen?"

"If they drive Cadillacs—could be. The redhead says Jeri had been bragging about driving her boy friend's Cad, and it so happens that Brother Curtis drives that very thing. But if you don't like it, forget it. Why don't we forget the whole business and just send flowers to the funeral?"

It was a lovely thought; but by this time Osgood had found that book of phone numbers and one of the business cards inside bore the name: *Arnold Fergus, M.D.* There couldn't be a funeral for quite a while now anyway.

The sign on the door said: *Saturday, 9 to 12,* and it was a couple of minutes past nine when Osgood walked in. All he wanted of Arnold Fergus, M.D., was a couple of direct answers to a couple of simple questions. Had he ever treated one Jeri Lynn, deceased? Had he ever prescribed a sedative of any type? It didn't seem such a lot to ask, but there was a distinct atmospheric change the moment he flashed his credentials.

Fergus was the athletic type. He was just changing into

his little white jacket when Osgood barged in, and those shoulders weren't padded. It seemed silly for such a big man to get nervous in front of a cop.

"Why—yes," he said to the first question. "I did treat Miss Lynn some months ago."

"Do you recall the complaint?"

"I believe so. She was in a general run-down condition. Overwork. Not enough rest."

"Too much night life?"

Doctor Fergus donned a pair of tortoise-rimmed glasses and sat down in the leather swivel chair behind his desk. He seemed more professional right away. "If I'm not mistaken," he said dryly, "night life was Miss Lynn's vocation. She was an entertainer in a night club just around the corner."

"I know all about that. What I'd like to know is the nature of your treatment. Specifically, did you ever give her a prescription for a barbiturate?"

It was as if Osgood had used a bad word. Even with his glasses on the doctor seemed to have difficulty finding his questioner's eyes, or, for that matter, anything else. The papers on his desk rattled furiously, and a note of annoyance crept into his voice.

"I really couldn't say offhand," he muttered. "As I told you before, it's been some time since I treated Miss Lynn."

"But you must keep records."

"Naturally—all the records the law requires and a few of my own as well. But I'm shorthanded this morning, Sergeant. My nurse is ill, and confound it, man, I can't seem to find a thing without her!" The papers rattled a noisy endorsement of his claim, and then, with an exasperated sigh, the doctor abandoned the desk-top search and rocked back in his chair. This time he actually looked at Osgood when he spoke.

"What's the trouble, officer?" he asked. "Do the police think Miss Lynn was a drug addict?"

Osgood wished people would stop planting notions in his head. First it was La Rene with that remark about the soldier, and now Dr. Fergus with another suggestion that could be just as troublesome.

"Was she?" he asked.

The doctor shrugged. "I'm not expert on such things. I'm just a general practitioner. But I've heard that addiction frequently occurs among persons in such arduous professions."

Strangely enough, now that Fergus had Osgood frowning he seemed in better spirits. Perhaps it was a case of perplexity loving company. "I'm sorry I can't be of more assistance," he added, as that busy look began to return, "but I'll have Miss Jenner get the information you want just as soon as she's able to come back to work. Now, if you don't mind, Sergeant, I have a patient coming in any moment—"

It was such a fast brush Osgood was almost to the door before the name hit home. "Miss Jenner," he repeated. "Would that be the same Miss Jenner who lives in that court where Jeri Lynn died?"

Such an innocent question, and yet it started all the papers rattling again. "Why, yes—I believe Miss Jenner does live in that court," he said vaguely. "But she's in no condition to be questioned. I've given her strict orders to remain in bed. Flu, you know. Terribly contagious."

"That's too bad," Osgood murmured. "Let's hope it doesn't develop into another epidemic that seems to be starting—loss of memory."

It was a shame to make Ann Jenner break the doctor's orders, but Osgood knew exactly where he was going when he left the medical center. Ann Jenner was the only occupant of that bungalow court who hadn't been interviewed, and in view of Jeri Lynn's condition a simple case of flu didn't seem so important. What's more, Dr. Fergus was a little too nervous for a man who should have acquired a more professional manner.

It was pretty early for any of Curtis Rathjen's night-blooming tenants to be up, and that double row of stucco looked as peaceful as Forest Lawn when he parked the sedan behind Tony Carmen's convertible. Osgood was traveling light. Frenchy had another errand to do, but Frenchy was still with him in a manner of speaking because he'd no more than hit the sidewalk than he noticed the big Cadillac sedan nosed into the driveway. He strolled over and read the initials on the door: C.R. At least that much of Frenchy's beauty-shop dirt was authentic. Then, just as he was trying to remember which apartment was Ann Jenner's, he became aware of a most interesting sight about halfway down the courtyard. Unless Rathjen had gone in for lawn statuary, that was a man with a small camera to his eye who posed facing the upstairs window. Fascinated, Osgood moved closer.

"Bird watching?" he queried, and the man almost fell backward over the low hedges.

It was the same little man of the rooftop. His camera was less conspicuous but not his fright, and that seemed a little peculiar since John Peter Osgood, even with his jaw stuck out, was in no way as terrifying as a hysterical Wilma Rathjen brandishing a knife.

"Now I've lost them," the little man whimpered. "I was trying to get the two of them together."

"The two of what? What are you hanging around here for anyway? What's so damned interesting about that roof?"

Questions seemed to be what the camera bug didn't like. For a moment he looked as if he intended to cut and run, but one of him faced with one of Osgood equaled encirclement. Then he seemed to remember something about a strong offense being the best defense. "Smart cop!" he muttered. "Got a crazy woman under your nose and don't know it!"

"I'm familiar with Miss Rathjen's background," Osgood said.

"Background! That's good! What about her foreground? Are you familiar with that?"

The man wasn't just standing there. He'd been groping through the pockets of his baggy tweed jacket like a tardy commuter hunting his ticket while the train pulls out, and now he came up with a glossy print that was shoved hurriedly into Osgood's hand.

"How do you like this for scenery?" he asked.

At first glance it wasn't much of a picture. Just a shot looking down on a lighted window—a bathroom window—showing a portion of the tub, a piece of the floor, and a corner of the doorway that led into an adjoining room; but it was the man who stood looking down into the tub that gave Osgood a delayed start.

"Hey, that's me," he cried. "Where did you get this?"

"From the roof. From the screwball's private roof. That's the shot she wanted to bust my camera for. Kind of interesting, isn't it? Just think, for two nights that window was lit up like this and the old girl didn't even notice the body in the tub. It's almost unbelievable!"

Almost! Osgood didn't wait to hear any more sarcasm. Curtis Rathjen or no Curtis Rathjen, the time had come for a few straight answers!

It was no pseudo insurance man who pounded up the stairs to Wilma's apartment, and it was no servile public employee who shoved past a protesting Curtis as if his sole function might be the opening of doors for angry policemen. He didn't slow down until he reached the wide front window. The whole courtyard spread out before him then—the courtyard and the window he'd come to see. The place was a regular crow's-nest. He must have been blind not to have realized that before.

He turned away from the window and found brother and sister Rathjen standing like a terrified Hansel and Gretel lost in the woods.

"Miss Rathjen," he said quietly, "why didn't you notify the police when you knew Miss Lynn was dead?"

CHAPTER TEN

There was going to be trouble, big trouble, and Wilma had known it all the time. She had no words for Osgood. Only a stricken face and one thin hand groping at her throat. It was Curtis who finally found his tongue.

"What's the meaning of this?" he demanded. "What right have you to come barging in here and make accusations against my sister?"

"I haven't made an accusation," Osgood said. "I merely asked a question."

"With no cause whatsoever!"

Curtis always talked too much when he was excited. Osgood silenced him by the simple means of shoving the photograph into his fat hand. "I'm still waiting for an answer, Miss Rathjen," he said.

Wilma tried to stand tall and proud, but there wasn't enough of her to stand tall, and she looked about as proud as a Christmas tree on the day after New Year's.

"How can I answer when I've no idea what you're talking about?" she said.

"You should know. Miss Lynn's body was in plain view from your window for two days."

"I work days."

"And two nights."

"I close my blinds nights! I only wish I could say as much for a few other people!"

"Jeri Lynn, for instance?"

Osgood wasn't smiling. The situation was much too

grim for that, but there was a certain brightness in his eyes that made Wilma afraid. She turned toward Curtis, but now Curtis was staring at her just as he'd done a few minutes earlier when he began to suspect what the sergeant now knew. Curtis and a policeman. It was just like that other time—Curtis and a policeman and then that terrible place—

"It's not true," she cried. "I didn't know she was dead. Curtis, tell Sergeant Osgood that it isn't true!"

But Curtis wasn't her brother any more. He was a stranger.

"You can't pay any attention to what my sister says or does," he said. "She's not responsible, Sergeant. She's not well."

"I am! I'm perfectly well!"

"Then stop lying!"

Curtis's words were like a slap across the mouth. Wilma sank back against the windowframe as if somehow, by some child's magic, she might become invisible. Stop lying! How could she stop lying when to tell the truth was to admit that she had doubted her own reason? If Curtis had stood by her, she might have bluffed the sergeant, but Curtis always had lost his head when he was cornered. It was the same when they were children and Papa reached for the strap.

Wilma sank back deeper and deeper, her wide eyes fastened on her brother's face as if he'd become the ghost of some long-departed dread. And then the child's magic worked, and she was invisible.

"She'll be all right," the nurse announced crisply. "She's had a nasty shock, but if we keep her quiet she'll be all right. What brought this on?"

Wilma drifted back from the dark cloak of invisibility and found that she was lying on her own divan with her own knitted afghan thrown over her and Ann Jenner's strong young hands tucking her in. The nurse wasn't in uniform, but even in a printed dress she had a professional air.

"What brought this on?" she repeated, and Curtis, with a wretched face, cleared his throat.

"All the excitement, I guess," he said.

"Excitement! Don't you realize that your sister is in no condition to stand excitement, Mr. Rathjen? What have you been saying to her?"

"What have *I* been saying to her!" Curtis's wound all but bled. "It's this blundering fool from the police department who's caused all the trouble! I don't recall seeing a warrant when you forced your way in here, Sergeant Osgood. I don't understand why you're haunting this place anyway. Why does it matter what my sister may or may not have seen?"

Curtis made it all sound very grim. Ann straightened up from arranging the afghan and stared at this man Osgood with new interest. *Sergeant* Osgood. Wilma could actually see the words form on her silent lips. It was still early and the girl wore no make-up, but such a healthy specimen shouldn't grow so pale just because the big man at the end of the divan was a police officer.

"I'm only trying to do my job," Osgood muttered. "I'm only doing what I get paid to do."

"By molesting a sick woman!" Curtis cried. "You don't have to tell me what you're paid to do, Sergeant. I'm a taxpayer!"

"So am I, Mr. Rathjen—and so was Jeri Lynn."

There was a big silence after Osgood's words, a heavy, listening silence as if there should be more to what he had said. Wilma opened her eyes wider and saw the way his big hands kneaded into angry fists, and then she measured his anger against Ann Jenner's lack of coloring. What the sergeant was saying—without words—was that Jeri Lynn's death was not a closed case. It was obvious where his suspicion centered, but Ann's pallor reminded Wilma of such significant things as the forgotten raspberry tarts and the rudeness of Dr. Fergus. She couldn't mention them, of course, or Curtis would accuse her of bearing tales again, but she had to do something to broaden the sergeant's point of view.

Suddenly Wilma sat bolt upright and stared at the nurse as if she'd never seen her before.

"What's this woman doing in my apartment?" she demanded. "Get her out! I don't want her here!"

It was a dangerous strategy laying her open to everything Curtis was already thinking; but she couldn't have gotten a better reaction with a pair of cymbals.

"Wilma, what are you saying?" Curtis cried. "Miss Jenner is here because I called her. She was kind enough to come when you fainted."

"I don't care. I don't want her here. She took care of Jeri Lynn when she was ill and now the poor girl's dead."

It was a terrible thing to say, especially when she didn't really know if Ann had done any such thing; but she did know Curtis well enough to realize what he must have done the night Jeri Lynn took ill. Curtis would have run for help to the nearest possible place, and that meant Nurse Jenner's apartment across the court. And her guess must have struck home. She could tell by the little gasping sound the nurse made, and the way her arms suddenly grew stiff at her sides. But she did make a quick recovery.

"I was afraid of something like this," she said (as if her words could wash away that sudden interest in the sergeant's eyes). "All the excitement that's been going on around here the past few days has completely unnerved the poor woman. Your sister needs a sedative, Mr. Rathjen. If you'll just stand by for a few moments, I'll run downstairs to my place and see—"

Wilma never understood why Ann Jenner broke off her speech so abruptly, or why Sergeant Osgood looked so alert. Perhaps there was a connection between the two events.

"I'll be glad to go downstairs for you, Miss Jenner," he said. "I suppose I'll find what you want in the bathroom."

"No, no, you won't!" Ann said quickly. "I was only going downstairs to use the phone. I think Miss Rathjen's physician should be called."

"Doesn't she have a phone?"

It was wonderful how it all worked out. Nobody even looked at Wilma any more, and the sergeant seemed to forget what he'd come for. He just stood there looking at the nurse in a puzzled sort of way, and then he looked almost happy over something Wilma couldn't understand at all.

"Why don't you call Doctor Fergus?" he suggested, on his way to the door. "He should be delighted to hear of your remarkable recovery."

Wilma wasn't the only person who couldn't understand. There was nothing new about people lying to John Peter Osgood. Certain types of people had been doing it since the day they first hung a badge on his shirt, and certain types of people could be persuaded to change their minds. But these weren't young punks or hoodlums he was dealing with now; they were nice, respectable pillars of society. That made their lies all the more interesting.

Wilma's denial was ridiculous, and something that would bear considerable looking into once brother Curtis had descended from the watchtower; but what really intrigued him, as he left that unhappy group behind, was the puzzle of a nurse too ill to report for duty and yet showing no signs of illness less than half an hour later. The only apparent reason for such byplay was to delay the surrender of Jeri Lynn's file from Dr. Fergus's office; but apparent reasons could be as phony as the issues in a political campaign. One way or another, young Dr. Fergus had some explaining to do, and it was still a long way from his twelve-o'clock closing.

That eager operator with the camera had vanished by the time Osgood reached the sidewalk again, but the old man in overalls was out early with his hedge' clippers. There were no hedges at the curbing, but a curious man wasn't going to be stopped by any such minor detail.

"Sure is a nervous woman," he remarked, nodding his shaggy gray head toward the garage. "What ails her this morning?"

There had been no rooftop screams on this occasion. "You must have been eavesdropping," Osgood said.

"Eavesdropping!" Timm spat his disgust on the sidewalk. "Live in this place and you can't help but eavesdrop. Walls like cardboard! When Rathjen phoned down to the nurse, it was like having the phone ring in my ear. I heard everything she answered."

"A situation like that could make life interesting," Osgood suggested, and the old man flashed a bargain-denture grin.

"Depends on who you got for neighbors. Now that blonde in back of me, she used to have some real interesting conversations until the phone company jerked out her phone. But the nurse is kind of a quiet one. The doctor used to call now and then, but not so much lately."

"Doctor Fergus?" Osgood asked.

"That's right. Know him?"

"I've met him. Nice-looking young man."

Timm nodded. "A widower with a little boy about five years old. Cute little fellow. The nurse is sure crazy about him."

"The little boy or the doctor?"

The bridgework grin came back again, and Timm reached into his back pocket for a yellow-stemmed pipe. "Well, now that you mention it, maybe both. I never pay much attention to that sort of thing."

The hell you don't, Osgood thought. Wallace Timm's blue eyes might have faded a little with the years, but they didn't miss much. These old codgers could be as bad as a back-fence gossip, and the way he constantly puttered about the place gave him plenty of opportunity to hear all, see all, and maybe, if he could be persuaded, tell all. He watched the old man fill the pipe and tamp it down with the stub end of what had once been a thumb, and it came to him that the knack of getting answers was to avoid direct questions and just let the old man's tongue wag in its natural fashion.

"It's too bad you don't live on the other side of the court," he suggested. "It might have been more interesting to have the apartment next door to the dead girl."

The match flame brightened Timm's eyes for an instant. "Why do you say that?" he asked.

"From what I hear, she wasn't so quiet."

Timm sucked on his pipe and worked up a big frown. Osgood didn't know whether that redness creeping up his neck was a sign of embarrassment or a slow burn. "People always talk about a pretty girl," he muttered. "People talk too damn much!"

"Maybe there's something to talk about."

"Sure, there's always something to talk about. Every one of us has things in our life we'd just as soon nobody remembered, but that don't make it right to stir up what's better left unstirred. Why do you want to hurt the boy? Ain't he suffered enough already?"

There was no doubt about the nature of that redness now. Osgood was as surprised as he was curious. "Boy?" he echoed. "What boy?"

"What boy! The boy she married, of course! Ain't it enough that he goes out and fights for his country and then comes back to find his wife dead? You can't change what's happened. You can't bring her back by stirring up a lot of dirt. All you can do is hurt the boy. He ought to have a little happiness left to him even if it's only a memory."

"Maybe he didn't have any happy memories," Osgood mused. "Not all marriages are, you know, even the three-day kind."

The old man looked at him as if he'd spit on the flag. "What crazy ideas have you got in your head?" he bellowed. "Of course he was happy. I remember."

"You remember what?"

"How happy he was—and the girl, too. It must have been right after the marriage, because I remember seeing him come here with Miss Lynn. I didn't think of it yesterday until after he told you who he was."

The old man was doing an awful lot of talking, and that thought must have occurred to him. He jammed the pipe back into his mouth and went back to the hedges. At the rate he was clipping the place would be denuded by nightfall. It seemed a shame to break up such an interesting conversation, so Osgood left the sedan and came back to where the old man was working.

"About Phillip Blade," he said, "he was here before Miss Lynn's illness, wasn't he? He was here while she was still working?"

"Where did you hear about Miss Lynn being sick?" the old man asked.

"From various places. I understand it was about six months ago."

"I guess it was. I don't remember dates very good."

"You knew about it, didn't you?"

"Of course I knew about it. Everybody living in the court couldn't help knowing. She took sick one night. Rathjen came running across the court yelling and pounding on the nurse's door to get Doctor Fergus. He'd noticed his car at the curb, I guess."

"Rathjen? Where was he running from?"

"The girl's apartment, of course. He'd come to collect

the rent, he said. Usually the agency does that, but sometimes Rathjen comes around just to check up on the place. Always raises hell, too. Nothing's ever right."

Wallace Timm went back to work with a vengeance, and the way he kept showing Osgood his back was a pretty good sign that he didn't intend to let his mouth run away with him again. Now and then he'd glance up at the apartment over the garage as if to see whether anyone was watching, and after a few minutes Curtis Rathjen came down the stairs with his bad humor marching like a herald before him.

"You just wait and see," Timm muttered half under his breath. "He'll find something to complain about."

But Osgood had seen enough of Curtis Rathjen for one morning. If this fount of information was really drying up, he might as well get on back to Fergus's office and demand an explanation that was beginning to seem a lot more important than Wilma Rathjen's window view anyway. But on the way over he switched on the radio and picked up a bulletin that took temporary priority over Fergus and his too healthy nurse.

CHAPTER ELEVEN

A couple of miles away from that run-down bungalow court filled with troubled people was one of the city's finest hotels filled with more troubled people. Not too long before Osgood heard about it, one of those troubled people was a certain Frenchy Bartel, who wasn't a registered guest or even a very pleasant visitor. He was just a policeman working his way through the answers of a beautifully groomed room clerk, a couple of porters, and a bartender who didn't like being called so early in the morning.

"When was the last time you saw him?" he asked again,

and the bartender groaned.

"I told you already! I don't know the time. About ten o'clock he came into the bar and started drinking. I recognized him right away from the newspapers, but I didn't say anything because he looked low enough without me butting in. I poured him a few drinks, three, maybe four, and then after a while I noticed he wasn't around any more. I didn't worry about it because the drinks went on the bill anyway. That's all I know."

That's all anybody knew, the room clerk, the porters, and anybody else Frenchy could buttonhole. But it wasn't all that Frenchy knew because he'd been having a busy morning, too. La Rene's suggestion was bearing fruit. He'd already learned that Phillip Blade's outfit had come in on the only troopship to dock locally all week, and the interesting thing about that item was that it had docked on Tuesday, not Friday. Tuesday morning, to be exact, just about eight hours before Jeri Lynn had taken her last bath. That left Pfc. Blade with a few important days to account for; but it seemed that Blade wasn't doing any accounting this morning. He had walked away from the hotel bar sometime after ten o'clock last night and hadn't been seen since.

This was the situation awaiting Osgood when he hurried back to headquarters, and it meant that he wasn't going back to that medical center after all. When it came to a choice of investigating a respectable young doctor, the sister of Curtis Rathjen, or an elusive Pfc., the decision wasn't hard to make. Everybody agreed there was something unnatural about a soldier delaying his homecoming for almost three days, especially when he had something like Jeri Lynn to come home to, and Pfc.'s couldn't cause any trouble if the lead turned sour and they resented the publicity.

Frenchy had a theory. According to the bartender in that hotel, Blade had been drinking alone, but that didn't mean a thing. A young soldier with overseas pay in his pocket wasn't going to stay lonely very long in this friendly city. He must have picked up a girl, or perhaps been picked up by a girl, and moved on to less formal surroundings to drown his sorrows.

And if the sorrow was murder?

"What of it?" said Frenchy. "Nobody was chasing. Why run?"

There was nothing wrong with the theory except that it meant a day of crawling through cheap hotels and low-class bars—the kind nobody but lower-echelon police officers and practically all the taxpayers seemed to know about, asking the same tired questions of the same tired people, and getting the same tired answers. It was the kind of day that could make Osgood wish he'd stayed in bed, and he might just as well for all the good that big crawl accomplished. The army only had a few million men in uniform, and this one had vanished like a raise in pay after taxes. By the time Osgood went off duty, headquarters knew no more about the whereabouts of Phillip Blade than they had when Frenchy brought in that first report. They did know a little more about the man himself. A check of his record showed a remarkable tendency for barroom brawls and a general belligerency above and beyond the call of duty, all of which added up to just about what Osgood had figured from the beginning: a hotheaded kid who could be handy with his fists without too much encouragement.

It was something to think about that night while soaking his feet and cursing the fate that had made him a policeman. How would a hotheaded kid go about disposing of an unfaithful wife? With a drug, a tub of water, and a hair dryer? Any such case he'd come across, and there were plenty, was more on the order of bare-hands or service-pistol technique. Maybe there was a point beyond anger that bred cunning, but Osgood had the uneasy feeling that the killer he was looking for wasn't quite so frank about his emotions. Of course, with no absolute proof that Jeri Lynn had been murdered, his speculation was a little premature; but in one busy day he'd seen Dr. Fergus have a memory failure, his nurse experience a miraculous recovery, and Wilma Rathjen faint dead away in the face of an obvious truth. It was getting so Osgood didn't care whether Jeri Lynn had taken Nembutal or cole slaw with her Scotch. When that many people ran for the hills, somebody had to be guilty of something.

But the city didn't pay Osgood to take his work home with him, so he turned on the television with the volume low (Ma was having another of her headaches) and tried to forget about four-cornered puzzles. It was about ten-thirty when the phone rang and spoiled his evening.

It sounded like a very happy place Frenchy was calling from. "If that redhead has a friend, the answer is no!" Osgood growled into the mouthpiece, but Frenchy had momentarily forgotten his hobby. He was at La Rene's doing a bit of relaxing when someone ran in yelling about a body out on the parking lot.

"There's a body, all right, but it's alive and groaning," he reported. "I thought you might be interested, Johnny. It's the old man, that hedge clipper from Rathjen's court."

Frenchy was right. Osgood *was* interested, and within fifteen minutes he was standing amid the Saturday-night bedlam of La Rene's kitchen with the lady herself pacing the floor like a bejeweled Captain Bligh with mutiny on her hands.

"Get this bum out of here," she roared, at the sight of Osgood. "What's this supposed to be, a receiving hospital?"

Wallace Timm looked as if he could use a hospital at that. They'd propped him up on a stool where he sat like a half-empty sack, one lapel of his threadbare jacket ripped loose, one eye closed, and an ugly bruise on his jaw that

Frenchy was swabbing with a dish towel.

"What happened?" Osgood asked, and Frenchy elevated one eyebrow.

"He fell down."

"How many flights?"

"That's what I asked him, but all he'll tell us is that he was out for a walk, took a short cut across the parking lot, stumbled, and fell down. Nobody knows what really happened because nobody saw him until he was out cold."

"I told you what happened," the old man broke in. "I had a dizzy spell and fell down."

"A customer of yours?" Osgood asked La Rene.

La Rene snorted like a Percheron with a heavy pull. "He comes in for a beer now and then," she said, "but he ain't been around tonight, if that's what you mean."

"That's right," Frenchy said. "He's got the breath of a baby, providing the baby smokes cheap cigars."

It didn't make sense. The old man was sober and in his right mind, and yet he expected them to believe he could be in that shape because he stumbled and fell on the parking lot. Maybe he was just too dazed to think of a good story, but why a story at all unless he was afraid to tell the truth?

But fear of what? Osgood looked at La Rene. Saturday night was a big production for La Rene, and here she was tied up with an unwanted convention in her kitchen. The only thing threatening about La Rene was her anxiety to see the meeting adjourn. Then he noticed one of the delegates he'd overlooked before, and that was remarkable since this bobby soxer's dream was all wrapped up in checks, tweeds, and Argyle socks.

"What are you doing here?" he asked Tony Carmen, and Tony shrugged.

"I helped carry him in," he said.

"You just happened to be on the premises, I suppose."

"That's right. I come around a lot, don't I, La Rene?"

"One of my best customers."

"What happened to your hand?"

Tony looked surprised, and then he glanced down at his right hand and the strip of tape stretched over the knuckles. "My God," he said, "I hope you don't think I hit the old man! Why should I?"

"Why should anybody?"

"How do I know? Maybe he had a date with a lady and she played rough."

"Women!" Timm snorted. "I don't waste no time on women! I fell down!"

"Anyway," Tony added, "I was at the bar all the time. Go on out and ask the bartender—he knows me."

"I'll take your word for it," Osgood said. "I only asked what happened to your hand."

"I cut it."

"Falling down?"

For just a moment Tony looked mad enough to throw a punch, and then he remembered that this was a cop he was talking to and a big one at that. So he grinned and all of those sparkling white teeth were beautiful. "I cannot tell a lie," he said. "I had an argument with a business associate."

"You shouldn't go around hitting horses," Frenchy remarked. "The S.P.C.A. will get you."

All the time Tony was talking Osgood kept his eyes on the old man's face, and he didn't seem particularly interested in either the source or what was being said. This whole business seemed to be just an annoyance to the old man, because whatever had happened out on the parking lot was his secret and no amount of questioning was going to have any effect on that stubborn jaw. Yet Osgood couldn't help thinking that it was rather strange that a man who had been so talkative a few hours ago could get antisocial in such a hurry.

Timm stood up and tried to walk on a pair of legs that

wobbled like a weak-kneed colt.

"You'd better let me take you to a doctor," Osgood said. "A blow on the head can be dangerous."

All he got for an answer was the old man's back as he tottered off toward the door. There wasn't a thing to do but take him home before he really did have a dizzy spell.

The court was as dark as a cemetery at midnight when Osgood helped Wallace Timm to his door. The only light showing was the long globe in the center arch, and it barely penetrated the shadows at the entrance to the courtyard. Apparently all the other tenants were either out on the town or had gone to bed—which was exactly what Osgood had in mind as soon as he got rid of his tongue-tied companion. But then he got to thinking that if someone had put the fear of the law into the old man, that someone just might return to see if the job had been effective. Certainly the court was dark enough to hide any would-be attacker.

There was no invitation to come inside, and no thanks for his trouble. The old man seemed to think the entire affair was a violation of his privacy. Maybe Tony was right, and the old boy had met a lady friend with Amazonian tendencies, but the thought didn't stop Osgood from making a quiet circuit of the court just the same. He followed the center walk to where it ran into the parking area in front of the garages, looked down the empty driveway that ran behind the south unit, and then checked the narrow gangway that led past the old man's back door to the street. The only sign of life he saw on the entire tour was the amber-eyed cat that watched his every move from the stair to Wilma Rathjen's apartment. He wondered if Alice got every night out, or if Saturday was an exception.

But there was nothing sinister about a cat, and so Osgood decided to let the old man worry about his own lumps and bruises and call it a day. He'd taken about six strides toward that lighted stucco arch at the front of the courtyard when a shadow broke out of the hedges and practically fell into his arms.

The startled cry from the captured shadow was little more than a sob, but Wallace Timm's door flew open to cut a bright wedge out of the darkness.

"Who is it? Who's out there?" he shouted.

"There's a man out here! He leaped at me!"

"A man? What man? Where?"

"Right here," Osgood said, pulling loose from a pair of clawing hands, "and I've never leaped at anybody in my life!"

But now the hands had a familiar face and figure behind them, and Osgood's protest faded to stunned surprise. It was Wilma Rathjen who was poised in that wedge of light like something that had to walk because she'd lost her broom.

"Oh, it's you!" she gasped. "Whatever are you doing here at this hour?"

It was a good question. Osgood had been about to ask it himself. "I took Mr. Timm home," he said. "He was hurt."

"I fell down," the old man said quickly.

Wilma's bright stare flew to the doorway for only an instant. She seemed much more interested in that narrow walk beyond Osgood's hulking shoulders. "If it was only a fall, you're fortunate," she said ominously. "After all the terrible things that have been going on around here, one never knows what to expect."

"Terrible things?" Osgood echoed. "What terrible things do you mean, Miss Rathjen?"

She looked at him as if he weren't quite bright. It was impossible to be sure in the darkness, but Osgood had the impression that she was concealing something behind the skirt of her short apron. The night was chilly, and yet she wore only a thin sweater for a wrap. It occurred to him then that this very probably wasn't Wilma Rathjen's street attire and that crawling about through the hedges at near midnight was a peculiar way of recuperating from the state in which he'd last seen her.

"What are you doing down here, anyway?" he asked.

Wilma blinked rapidly. "I thought I saw a prowler," she said. "I came down to investigate."

"A prowler? That's peculiar. I've been here in the court-yard ever since I brought Mr. Timm home, and I haven't seen anyone."

"Oh, it was before that. It was before you came."

"You can't pay any attention to anything she says," Wallace Timm objected. "She's always seeing things that ain't there."

It was a brave statement coming from a man obligated to Wilma Rathjen's brother. From the sergeant she could expect trouble, but not from this underling. "Is that so?" she cried. "I suppose I imagined that Jeri Lynn was dead! I suppose I imagined that man at the bathroom window!"

"Man?" Osgood echoed. "What man are you talking about?"

There was a moment when nobody spoke and nobody moved. Wilma stood imprisoned in that frame of doorway light. Wallace Timm was to the right of her; Sergeant Osgood was straight ahead of her. The sudden anger fled from her eyes, but it was too late to call back her words.

"What man?" Osgood repeated, and the whole night seemed to listen for her answer.

"I must be getting upstairs," Wilma said. "It's really quite late and tomorrow is church—"

"Miss Rathjen, I asked you a question!"

It was foolish to try to scurry past him. The walk was narrow, and Osgood's reach was long. Her arm was like a child's in his big hand. She seemed to have no flesh at all. "You can't go by anything she says," Timm called out again, but now he was just the forgotten man in this episode because Osgood intended to get a straight answer for a change even if he had to take Curtis Rathjen's sister down to headquarters and throw the book at her. And then, without any warning at all, Wilma did the only thing she could do with the inevitable.

"As long as you're here, Sergeant," she said, in a calm and measured voice, "perhaps you will be kind enough to see me upstairs. I seem to have forgotten to leave a light, and I do so dread going into a dark apartment alone."

Anything could happen. If the events of a crowded day hadn't convinced Osgood of that truth, Wilma's quick change of attitude was sufficient to turn the trick. One moment he was a black inquisitor blocking her way to safety, and in the next he was Sir Galahad in dark-gray worsted escorting a lady to her door. And he didn't stop at the door. Invitation or no invitation, this time he intended to tag her heels until she explained herself. But that foot in the door was totally unnecessary. Wilma almost smiled as she beckoned him inside.

"I know it's terribly late," she said, "but then you are an officer of the law, and I hardly think anyone in this court is in a position to criticize."

There was a kind of sorry acceptance in Wilma's manner, as if everything had been settled down in the courtyard a few moments earlier. A tongue had slipped, a revelation had been made, and now certain things must be said to this persistent policeman. She moved across the room with one hand still held under her apron and a perplexed frown troubling her forehead.

"I think a cup of chocolate would be nice," she mused. "Do you drink chocolate, Sergeant?"

"There's no need to bother—" Osgood began.

"Oh, it's no bother. I'll have it ready in a jiffy. Just make yourself at home."

Osgood started to protest and then changed his mind. He still wanted to know about that man at the bathroom window, but the last time he'd tried forcing this woman, she retaliated by falling into a faint. He wanted no more of that. And she couldn't duck out. The kitchen was little more than an alcove separated from the living-room by a pair of shutter screens. It had no exit of its own. He heard the cupboard doors open and close, and then the busy sounds of pots and pans and trips to the refrigerator. Such hospitality was a new side of Wilma Rathjen. He seemed to find a different woman each time they met.

But what had she been doing down in those hedges? He walked over to the front windows and tilted the shutters so he could look down into the courtyard below. The old man's light had gone out, and that made the darkness unanimous except for that lone globe in the stucco arch. Remembering her history, he reflected that there were no bright windows to spy upon and no antics to watch.

"Would you care for cookies with your chocolate, Sergeant?"

The unexpected query brought Osgood back from the window in a hurry.

"They're awfully good," Wilma added. "From the bakery, you know."

She was setting a tray full of blue-and-white-china pieces down on the cobbler's bench, and if she'd disapproved of his window stance, it wasn't evident in her narrow face. She was much too preoccupied admiring her chocolate set.

"Aren't they lovely pieces?" she murmured. "Royal Copenhagen. They were my mother's, but she willed them to me."

"Very nice," Osgood muttered.

"Of course, it's only right that she left them to me. By rights she should have left everything to me. I waited on her hand and foot for almost twenty years. She was an invalid, you know."

Osgood hadn't known. This small, unstudied confession was the first thing of interest that he'd heard since entering the apartment.

"A bedridden invalid," she added. "I took care of her and the house, and then, after Father died, I took charge of selling the farm— But, then, I suppose Curtis needed his share, what with an extravagant wife and two children to support."

It was strange what a difference a few words could make when it came to trying to understand Curtis Rathjen's sister. Osgood was the perfect guest now. He sat down on the edge of the divan and held a dainty chocolate cup in his hand as if it contained a small explosive that might go off at any moment. Wilma faced him from the cricket chair.

"I do hope you weren't offended at my boldness in asking you to come upstairs with me," she remarked, "but I didn't want Wallace Timm to hear my confession. I'm not at all sure that I trust that man."

As casually as that! Osgood was wrong about the chocolate; the explosion was in his windpipe.

"Confession?" he gasped.

"Yes, confession. I lied to you this morning. I did look out of my window. I've known since Tuesday night that Jeri Lynn was dead."

It was several heartbeats before Osgood could speak, and then he demanded the whole story, and she told him in a voice that was neither agitated nor depressed. She'd worked later than usual, until seven at least. "It was my night to close, and I'm not very good at checking out. I'm not very good at anything, I'm afraid. I make mistakes. I order things and the customers never come, and then Mrs. Waggoner says it's all my fault and reports me to the supervisor. That's why I had to take—" The voice died away for a moment. "That's why I have to be so careful," she added.

"And was the girl dead when you reached home?"

"I really don't know. The light was on in her bathroom when I came home, but I didn't think anything of it then. It was later, when I let Alice out, that I became curious. Even a girl like Jeri Lynn wouldn't primp so long—" Wilma's voice fell away to silence, and then she shuddered. "The next day she was still there, and the next. I thought they would *never* find her!"

"But, Miss Rathjen, why didn't you notify the police?"

It was the same question that had started all the trouble on Osgood's morning visit, but he couldn't hold it back any longer. And this time the woman didn't faint. She looked straight into his eyes, and a sad shadow of a smile touched her lips.

"I called the police once," she said. "I saw something I thought was wrong and reported it to the police, but I was mistaken. I didn't want to be mistaken like that again. I would rather be dead."

There was no emotion in her voice. She punctuated her words with quick sips of chocolate and went on in that terrible quiet tone.

"They took me to a horrible place, and I had to stay there for months and months with a lot of vulgar, dirty women. I couldn't even have my own room. I couldn't even have a place where I could go and shut the door."

"That's all over now," Osgood said quickly. "You have a real nice place here."

"Yes, it is nice, isn't it?" The memories receded from Wilma's haunted eyes, and she looked about her with the proud smile of possession. "I bought all the pieces myself with what Mother left me when she died. I studied the magazines and bought just the right things even if they were expensive. It was the dream of my life to have just a little place of my own."

It was easy to listen to the woman and be carried away on a swell of uneasy sympathy; but John Peter Osgood was still a policeman even with a cup of chocolate in his hand. "What about that man at the bathroom window?" he reminded, and the mood of the conversation changed instantly.

"Oh, that was later, Sergeant. That was Thursday night after the body had been removed. I let Alice out about midnight and saw a man standing outside Miss Lynn's bathroom window watching the light."

"What light?" Osgood demanded.

"The flashlight. There was another man inside the apartment—no, I don't really know that it was a man. It could have been Ann Jenner. "

She couldn't get away with dropping a casual reference like that. Now Wilma had to tell about the nurse's reaction to the news of Jeri Lynn's death, and fill in all the details about the prowlers—even to showing him that carefully preserved cigarette butt in the top desk drawer. All the time she watched Osgood's face for signs of credulity, and all the time he watched hers for signs of what could be believed.

"And now she's run away," Wilma said.

"Miss Jenner?"

Wilma nodded. "Not an hour after you left us this morning. I watched from the windows. First I saw Tony Carmen leave in a frightful state of anger—I could tell by the way he slammed the door behind him and raced the motor when he drove away. Then, about ten minutes later, Doctor Fergus came for the nurse and they drove off together. She was carrying an overnight bag."

"Maybe she went off on a case."

A vague smile called Osgood naïve. "She wasn't wearing her uniform," Wilma said.

At least Osgood had what he'd come for and a little more besides, and it was just as he'd thought in the courtyard—anything could happen! It was a lot to digest on top of a cup of chocolate. He couldn't argue with the woman's excuse for not reporting the girl's death—it was the kind of inverse reasoning that would seem logical to her. But if she'd lied in the morning she might have started lying a lot earlier. The thought had no more than crossed his mind when she intercepted it.

"I realize that I should have told you all this sooner," she said, "but I couldn't speak in my brother's presence. He's so excitable when I do something wrong. And at the time I saw those prowlers I still thought Miss Lynn's death was accidental."

"And you don't think so now?"

Wilma seemed to enjoy the response in Osgood's eyes. She smiled like a hostess whose party has gone well.

"Do you, Sergeant Osgood?" she asked.

CHAPTER TWELVE

Osgood didn't answer Wilma's question. The conversation was reaching the point where he wasn't quite sure who was questioning whom, so he made a hasty exit and left the woman to puzzle things out for herself. He left the court by the center walk, and Wilma, watching from behind a tilted shutter, was gratified to see that he didn't stop to examine the hedges she'd been climbing through or look at the window behind them. It was so easy to break into these old apartments. The French windows never closed right after the rains, and few of the screens had locks— He was gone at last. She closed the blind tight and trotted back to the kitchen. The excuse of making a pot of chocolate could come in handy when a person wanted to get rid of something a policeman shouldn't see. She opened the top cupboard and took out that strange thing she'd found in the woman's apartment. Perhaps she should have shown it to the sergeant after all—he would have believed her insinuations then! But what of Curtis? Curtis had warned her against making trouble for any of his precious tenants, and Curtis was more to be feared than any policeman.

But it was such a despicable thing! A wave of anger swept over Wilma as she looked at it again—a disgrace, an insult to her sex! Hardly realizing what she was doing, she ripped the offensive object in two and started to stuff it inside the cake box in readiness for the incinerator in the morning. And then she drew back her hand. Why had the woman kept such a photograph in her desk unless she was guilty? Perhaps Curtis could explain that.

Despite her midnight decision, Wilma didn't get the cake to the incinerator after all. It was Sergeant Osgood's fault. The shock he'd given her in the courtyard and the difficult time she'd had trying to talk herself out of a corner weren't sleep-inducing. It was dawn before she slept at all, and the sun was high in the heavens when she finally awakened to the hush of a Sunday morning.

Sunday morning was the loveliest time of Wilma's life, the one shining light at the end of each weary week. On Sunday she wore her finest. With trembling hands she would undo the paper covers and examine each precious garment for signs of soil and wear. She could never abide soiled clothing—that was one of the things that had been so terrible about that place they sent her when she was sick. Nothing was ever quite clean and nothing was ever private. Any one of those dirty women might wear her things and spoil them. That was all behind her now, but sometimes she couldn't be sure. Sometimes she didn't recall a powder stain or recognize the scent of stale cologne.

The reason for all this Sunday morning preparation was, of course, Wilma's church. The service was the oasis from which she was refreshed in the desert of an alien world. The service was what heaven must be. The organ played, the hymns rose to God, and sometimes it seemed she could actually see the white-robed Jesus standing on the platform with his arms outstretched. Once, and this she had never confided even to Curtis, she had seen her mother standing beside Him, straight and whole now that she had shuffled off that sinful, pain-racked body! It was an hour of ecstasy after which she emerged from the house men had built for God to walk with fear and revulsion in the house God had built for men.

But there would be no such hour this Sunday. As soon as she realized the time Wilma dressed hurriedly in her housekeeping cotton. The burning must be over by ten according to a city ordinance, and on Sundays old man Timm always collected the wastebaskets from the downstairs apartments and burned the contents. He would monopolize the incinerator for hours, and she wanted no audience for her task. But with all her hurrying she was too late. From the roof deck she could look down and see the old man feeding the flames like a child might feed animals at the zoo. The wastebaskets were his particular delight. It seemed to be such fun to see what the other tenants had thrown away.

She watched him for a long time. It was going to be too late, she knew. She'd have to keep that cake another day. The fire died lower, and the last wastebasket stood empty, but still the old man didn't move away. He stood there in a pair of cotton trousers that seemed to be always in a half crouch and poked at the sinking fire with a long stick, and then he did a strange thing. He took a letter from his shirt pocket and turned it over in his hands. Then he took out the sheets of paper and read them over again. (It appeared to be a letter that had been read many times.) Next, with a kind of shrug, he tossed the letter into the fire and helped it along with the stick until it was burned. Wilma noted all this before she finally turned away.

The day had begun badly. The cake wasn't burned, the beautiful service was missed for nothing, and when she tried to call Curtis to tell him about what she had found on her nocturnal excursion, she could get only a servant with an impatient voice. A dark anger began to well up in Wilma's heart against these troublesome tenants who spoiled so many plans and created so many sleepless nights. She could see more of them now in the courtyard below. They came out with the sun like snakes on a mountainside. They came out half naked and unashamed. She walked to the front of the roof deck and glared down at the Sunday-morning orgy in the grass. Tony Carmen was already out in his yellow trunks, and just as she approached the rail, he emitted a low whistle at the theatricals, who were posing in brief sun suits for some young friend with a box camera. It was disgusting! They had no modesty at all, Wilma thought as she glared down at both of them.

Suddenly the anger was too much for Wilma to contain. "You girls should be ashamed of yourselves!" she cried out. "Why don't you take everything off the way that other one did? You're all of a kind!"

The stunned silence that followed her outburst—and Wilma was the most stunned of all—was broken by the sound of giggles. Wilma began to back away from the railing, but Tony Carmen wasn't giggling. Tony was on his feet and coming toward her with an upturned face filled with quick anger.

"What do you mean by that?" he shouted. "Hey, you old witch, come back here!"

Wilma turned and fled into her apartment. She hadn't meant to cry out that way. Now she had made a fool of herself in front of all those people. She could hear their laughter and Tony's grumbling threat: "Some day she'll snoop once too often and get a bloody nose!" and leaned back against the door trembling on the verge of tears. Curtis would hear of it and be angry again, and he'd never believe where she found that photograph.

The beautiful Sunday was ruined. The sunshine looked dirty now—everything looked dirty. She had no idea the apartment was in such a deplorable state.

Wilma wasn't the only one who had trouble with Sunday. For Ruby Lennox the day was real grief. It wasn't only the memories and the melancholy; it was mostly because Sunday had to come after Saturday night. Ruby was thinking about that as she struggled up the stairs to Wilma's apartment. Each step was like butting her head in a wall, but it was getting on toward six o'clock, and she was never going to make it to work. At the top of the stairs she paused to recover her breath and then she began to pound on Wilma's door. Somebody in this damn court had to be at home!

"Hi, Miss Rathjen," she said, when Wilma finally opened the door. "Hope I didn't spoil a nap or anything."

Wilma didn't look as if she'd been napping. She had a dustcloth in one hand and a bright piercing stare in her eyes.

"I was wondering, could I use your phone? The company yanked mine the other day, and I gotta call the boss. I tried everybody downstairs and they're either all out or dropped dead."

Ruby chuckled at her own wit in an appreciation Wilma didn't share, but she did unhook the screen door. There wasn't much else she could do.

"The phone is on the desk," she said.

"Oh, sure. I won't be a minute."

Ruby hadn't bothered to dress all day. She was wearing a short terry-cloth robe, and Wilma could only hope there was something underneath, but with a woman like Ruby

Lennox she could never be sure. She didn't want to look at her. She didn't want to listen in on that conversation, either, but it was difficult to avoid in an apartment so small. Ruby dialed a number and sat down on the edge of the desk.

"Hello, Papa," she said thickly. "Say, you better get yourself another hasher for tonight. Little Ruby'll never make it.... What? Hell, no! I ain't sick, honey. I just lifted a few too many this afternoon. This drinking alone is rough. There's nothing to do between drinks."

Ruby laughed riotously, and Wilma began to polish the cobbler's bench with a vengeance. She'd been over the living-room already, but she didn't want to leave this woman alone. Soon she would finish her call and get out—that's what she must remember. Soon she would be gone.

But Ruby was in no hurry. She slammed the phone back on the cradle and just sat there on the edge of the desk watching Wilma's labors.

"Well, ain't you got the energy!" she said. "You sure do keep this place spic and span. Expecting someone?"

It was just like Ruby Lennox to think an apartment never needed cleaning unless company was coming. When Wilma set her straight, Ruby sighed sympathetically.

"Ain't it hell being alone on Sunday?" she said. "Seems like everybody else in the world has got something to do, go to the beach, go to a show, take the kids for a ride."

Ruby was beginning to look misty-eyed. Wilma wasn't sure whether or not this was a manifestation of alcoholism.

"I wish I had a kid to take somewhere," she added wistfully. "I never had much fun when I was a kid. My old man was potted half the time and, Jesus, he was a mean one!"

Ruby got off the desk top and started moving toward the door, but she never moved anywhere very fast.

"I'll bet you never had much fun when you were a kid, either," she added. "Just like me."

The thought of being like Ruby Lennox in any respect frightened Wilma into response. "I was brought up properly!" she protested.

"Yeah, I know what you mean. But what the hell, we're better off not thinking about it. How could I keep a kid on six bits an hour anyway?"

Ruby yawned and stretched in a writhing movement. "You wouldn't catch me working all day if I lived in a quiet place like this," she added. "You should have old man Timm next door muttering and fussing all the time. He must be going nuts, talking to himself!" Then she grinned and went to the door. "Like I'm doing now. Thanks for the use of the phone, Miss Rathjen, and don't wear yourself out with that dustcloth."

At last she was gone! Wilma slammed the door and locked it, and then she went to work dusting off the desk top....

There was no use trying to clean any more. The dirt accumulated faster than it could be removed. She'd been over the rugs half a dozen times, dusted until her arms ached, and scrubbed until her fingers were raw. Now she sat in the darkness so she couldn't see the dirt come back. It was a frightening thing, and she didn't want to be alone.

The last two times she'd tried to call Curtis, Katherine answered. She tried to explain, but Katherine didn't understand. "Ask Curtis to call me when he comes in," she said finally, and the woman promised, but Wilma didn't believe her. Katherine didn't like her because of the way she'd disgraced them all that time with the police. She even thought of calling Sergeant Osgood, who should have frightened her more than anyone but didn't. Maybe that was because there were so many other things to fear. With her hand on the receiver she remembered that she couldn't do that. Sergeant Osgood was a policeman, and the police always wanted a name for fear. There should be some place people could call who were just afraid of being afraid.

It was Alice playing a cat's-paw solo on the screen door that finally brought Wilma out of the darkness. "All right, kitty, I'll let you in," she called out. On her way to the door she pressed the switch and all of the lamps responded with light. She wasn't going to look at the room any more. She was just going to let Alice in, feed her, and get right to bed— And then all the lights went out at once.

For a moment Wilma expected to die. There was a demon from hell in her apartment—what else could have done that to the lights? She even felt it brush against her skirts as she stood in the open doorway, and there was no time to consider whether it might not have been the cat. A demon from hell was nothing to toy with. Since she hadn't died, she had to run; and the only place to run was toward that light showing at the foot of the stairs. It didn't matter which apartment the light came from or whose startled face answered her frantic clawing at the door.

"The lights!" Wilma cried. "The lights!"

There was something wrong with Ruby's lights, too, but that had nothing to do with the electric company.

"They've all gone out!" Wilma insisted. "Can't you see? My lights have all gone out!"

"If they've gone out how can I see?" Ruby muttered, but then through a mellow haze she began to see the picture Wilma painted in such vivid hues. The lights had gone out, and the old girl thought someone was in her apartment. It was funny, and it was sad all at the same time.

"You poor old soul," Ruby said, throwing an arm about her narrow shoulders. "You're up there alone all the time, ain't you? I think it's stinkin' the way your brother treats you!"

"But the lights—"

"Sure, they went out. You told me. That's nothin' to get so scared about, honey. You just blew a fuse, that's all."

Ruby had one standard prescription for any kind of trouble. She stumbled over to the sink and poured a shot glass full of whisky from an almost empty bottle. "Here, you drink this," she said, pushing the glass into Wilma's hand. "You just sit down and drink this and old Ruby will fix everything. Now where the hell's my flashlight?"

Wilma began to feel foolish. A fuse! Why hadn't she thought of that? The fuse box was on the far side of the garage where any of the tenants could get to it without disturbing the others, and she could go out and flip the little lever as well as Ruby. But she made no move to follow Ruby out. The fear was still too near and the darkness too terrible. She looked down at the glass of whisky in her hand and put it down on the nearest table with a grimace of disgust. After that she just waited for Ruby to come back.

It was at least fifteen minutes before she worked up enough courage to walk down to the fuse box and see what was taking the woman so long. By that time Ruby was dead.

CHAPTER THIRTEEN

Wilma found her crumpled in a heap on the cement slab just below the fuse box. The flashlight was broken, but there was just enough moonlight to make out that white terry-cloth robe and the silver-blond hair that was now matted with a dark stickiness that had to be blood. She knew right away that Ruby was dead. It seemed, somehow, as if she'd almost expected to find her this way, as if this was what the tension of the day had been working up to all the time. Ruby was dead, and on the cement beside her was a flat strip of iron with the same dark stickiness on one end. Poor Ruby. If only she hadn't gone out to flip the switch—

Suddenly Wilma was trembling with fear. It was her lights that had gone out. She was the one who should have come to the fuse box to meet death. She backed away from the body and crouched against the side of the garage. What was out there in the night? Who was waiting to kill Wilma Rathjen? Somewhere a dog barked, and somewhere a door banged shut. Somewhere there were footsteps on the cement walk. She wanted to run to the stairs and hide inside her own apartment, but all this time the door had been standing open, and all this time there was no light. Now her sanctuary seemed a deathtrap, and every sound in the night was danger. There was nothing to do but run.

The boulevard on a Sunday night was about as lively as a cemetery drive. There were street lights and neons—even a few lighted windows—but none of the doors were open, and nobody walked the streets. Wilma wouldn't have dared stop anyone if there had been anyone to stop, for now the fear was growing into a giant with a masked face. Somewhere death was waiting to rectify its error, and she had no more idea of who that killer might be than of why she was supposed to die. She ran wildly and without direction, and then suddenly she was in the midst of a great many people.

"Hey, watch it, lady!"

That was the man who pushed Wilma off his shirt front. Behind and beside him were a lot of other shirt fronts and low-bosomed gowns. None of them had any faces that Wilma could see; they were just a moving mass of people pouring out of a bright foyer; someone laughed as she righted herself; someone even called out, "They went that-away!" as she pulled free and ducked down an alleyway away from the crowd. But the alley was a dead end, and she was trapped in a rectangle of light.

"Why, Miss Rathjen! Whatever are you doing here?"

Wilma spun about and found Denise staring at her from the open doorway. Now she understood. This was the little playhouse and she'd come straight to the stage door.

"My—my cat!" she gasped. "I'm looking for my cat. She ran away."

"All the way up here?"

Wilma couldn't think of any other alibi, and she couldn't scoot away fast enough to avoid Denise's quick grasp.

"Why, you're trembling," the girl said. "You've come a without a coat!"

"But my Alice—"

"Now, don't you worry about Alice. She'll come home. You just come in here, and I'll get you something to wear home."

For a little girl Denise had a lot of strength, and Wilma was fresh out. She felt herself being pulled into a bright bedlam of backstage activity. Young men in T shirts and tight denims were shouting to one another over trunks and backdrops, and a great many people with painted faces were crowding into the dressing-rooms. That was where Denise took Wilma, to a dressing-room teeming with half-naked girls getting out of their make-up and into their costumes. One of the girls was Sharl, and her mouth dropped open at the sight of Wilma.

"Miss Rathjen!" she cried. "What gives?"

Wilma didn't catch the head-shaking signal Denise passed behind her back. She was too busy getting shoved out of the way behind a loaded costume rack. "You just sit there on the stool until I get my clothes changed," Denise ordered, "and then Sharl and I will walk you home." Denise melted back into the crowd of girls before Wilma could open her mouth in protest. Home was the last place she wanted to go now! Home was where the danger was, and now that she had a moment to think, that danger was double. She was responsible for Ruby Lennox's death. One way or another she was responsible, and could there be any doubt of what way the police would choose? There was a dark stain on her right hand—Ruby's blood; perhaps her fingerprints were on that iron strip—she couldn't remember.

But how far could she run? Hatless, coatless, penniless—within an hour every policeman in the city would have a word picture of so conspicuous a fugitive. She shrank back against the wall, but none of those chattering girls seemed to know or care that she was there. Then one of them came toward her carrying a fiery-red wig in her hands.

"Am I glad to get rid of this thing!" she muttered. "It's not only hot. It itches."

From across the room came a sarcastic taunt: "Are you sure it's the wig that itches?" and Wilma immediately found herself sitting on the edge of a battle of temperaments with a fiery-red wig in her lap. She picked it up and scooted the stool behind the costume rack. Maybe there was a way out after all. If only that battle lasted long enough she might make a few changes of her own. She began to grab wildly from the rack. A green velvet coat, a cheap white fur piece, a pair of green satin shoes from the shelf. Now and then she peeked out between the costumes to see if anyone was watching, but apparently a full-blown feud was developing. She chanced a trip to an abandoned dressing table for a quick application of lip rouge and powder, and then the wig—

Nobody noticed when Wilma sneaked out of the theater. Nobody would have recognized her if they had.

Wilma Rathjen had a new wardrobe and a new face, but she had no place to go. The green shoes had high heels and after a few blocks they began a kind of crippling torture, but she had to walk because she had no money for carfare. She walked toward town, toward the lights and the clubs and the people, because it was easier to get lost among people than on a lonely residential street. It was also easier to call for help if a killer emerged from the shadows.

After a while the pain was too much, and Wilma took off her shoes and walked with them in her hands. She walked with her eyes on the sidewalk, hoping that she might find even so much as a dime with which to telephone Curtis, but all she found were bottle caps and pebbles to cut her stockinged feet. Once she passed a sedan that had stopped for the signal and heard the riotous laughter of the people inside. One of them, seeing the shoes in her hand, leaned out the window and yelled, "Take it off, take it off!" It was enough to drive Wilma back into the shadows—and back into her shoes.

She walked a long time. The street became noisy and bright with neons. Now there were people coming and going from the black-mouthed bars, and once in a while the sound of wild, primitive music blared out from some alcoholic den of iniquity. The night was evil. The night, the street, the faces in the street, the whole world was evil and she had to get away! But to do that she must have money. And then she spied a taxi with the driver sitting inside reading a newspaper by the light of a street lamp.

"Taxi!" she cried.

The driver raised his head from the newspaper and looked her over from head to foot.

"Beat it!" he said.

"But I want to engage your cab. I want to go to my brother's house."

There were at least forty years of cynicism on the cab driver's swarthy face. He stared at the freakish exhibit before him and sighed. This wasn't the kind of fare he relished. An old one like this never had any money; he'd be lucky to get a dime tip.

"Where does your brother live?" he asked, reaching for the door handle. When Wilma told him, he kept his hand on the handle. "Bel Air?" he echoed. "You got a brother in Bel Air? What does he do, mow the lawn?"

It was almost too much. Wilma had to bite her tongue to keep from giving the man the comeuppance he deserved, but just in time she remembered how angry Curtis would be if she used his name. Especially in a getup such as she was wearing! She was trying desperately to think of some way to convince the man when something in the street made that impossible. A police car rounded the nearest corner and came slowly toward them. Wilma didn't dare stay under the street lamp with the police around. For all she knew they might be looking for her even now. She scurried for the nearest dark doorway, and the cab driver's laughter followed her all the way. Before she could come out again, he had driven off with another fare.

And so it came back to the problem of money again. She must have money, but how does one go about raising money on an evil street in the middle of a Sunday night? Money was raised through banks and bonds and selling things— That was it! Selling things! She wore one piece of jewelry, an opal ring set in gold. She'd never meant to part with it as long as she lived because it had been her mother's ring, but perhaps she could borrow money on it and redeem it later. But again it was Sunday night. Who loaned money on a Sunday night? There wasn't anything open but those terrible saloons. She walked slowly, keeping close to the buildings and watching for police cars on the street, and after a while she stopped at one of the black mouths with the loud music and evil smell and went inside.

Never in all her forty-three years had Wilma been in such a place. She stood just inside the door for a moment waiting for her eyes to become adjusted to the darkness and her knees to stop shaking. At any moment she expected to be grabbed and attacked in the darkness, but nobody seemed to be aware of her entrance. Just ahead was a round counter with a raised platform inside. On the platform three perspiring Negroes were coaxing weird sounds out of a trumpet, a piano, and a drum. Spaced on stools around the outside of the counter were a few shadowy figures, mostly men, and inside the counter a pair of white-jacketed employees were pouring drinks from the elaborate array of bottles on the shelves behind them. There were a few booths along one side of the room, and Wilma had to pass some of them to reach the counter. She was afraid to look at the people sitting in the booths. She was afraid of what she might see.

"All right, lady, what's yours?"

Wilma had gone to the farthest end of the bar because most of the people were sitting nearer the door. She wanted a private talk with the proprietor.

"Are you the manager?" she asked timidly.

"I'm the manager of this bar," the man in the white jacket said. "Now what's yours?"

"Oh, I don't want a drink. I want to speak to you about a matter of business."

The bartender eyed her just as the cab driver had done, and then his face got ugly. "Oh, no, you don't!" he said. "We don't have any of that in here! This is a respectable place!"

Wilma had no idea what the bartender was talking about. She'd taken the ring from her finger and was holding it up in a timid, desperate gesture. "But it's a genuine opal," she insisted. "It belonged to my mother."

"What belonged to your mother?"

"This ring. That's what I want to talk to you about. If I could just have a few dollars tonight my brother will redeem it tomorrow."

"Migawd," the bartender said, "you must be thirsty!"

"But I don't want a drink! I just want a few dollars for

a taxi."

Wilma never did understand what was so funny, but suddenly the man in the white jacket was laughing and telling his companion that he'd never heard this one before, and then what he was saying raced along the counter until everybody began to chuckle and stare. It was too much. The whole day, the terrible night, they were just too much. She felt a tightness in her throat and then the tears came in a deluge. It was horrible to weep that way with her head on the bar and all those awful people laughing at her, but then suddenly they weren't laughing, and the man in the white jacket was patting her arm and pleading with her not to take it so hard.

"Okay, okay," he said. "Let me see the ring again."

There was a murmur of assent along the bar. Wilma had the feeling the people would have been angry if he hadn't said that. He took the ring and carried it over to the light. "It doesn't look like much to me," he said, "but if you're sure your brother will come in tomorrow—"

"Oh, he will!" Wilma cried. "I wouldn't want to part with that ring. It was my—"

"Yeah, I know, it was your mother's." The man in the white jacket came back and pulled a five-dollar bill from his trouser pocket. "This was going to be my wife's," he muttered, "and she wouldn't want to part with it, either. Now please, lady, go home."

His voice was rough, but his face wasn't ugly any more. It was all very strange.

There were no taxis on the street. It might as well have been raining because there were no taxis anywhere. Wilma held the five dollars in one tight fist and started walking again. The tears had broken the tension that had carried her on. Now she could hardly move one foot before the other. She should have asked the man in the white jacket to call a cab, but after all that fuss it seemed an imposition.

After all, he wasn't a jeweler; he couldn't know but what the ring was a fake and he'd never see his money again. She wanted to cry again and just go on crying, and then she wanted to sleep.

She passed the dark window of a Western Union office, and the clock in the window told her it was after one o'-clock. Curtis wouldn't like being awakened at this hour, and Curtis wouldn't like the way she looked or what she had done. Then a terrible thought came like icy fingers on her heart. Curtis wouldn't trust her the way the bartender had. Curtis wouldn't believe anything she said. It would take arguing and pleading, and she was too tired. Tomorrow, maybe tomorrow she could go to Curtis. Tonight she wanted only to blot out the terrible nightmare with sleep.

Across the street lights were burning in the lobby of a cheap hotel. It might not be clean or respectable, but somehow that didn't matter. At least she'd have something left from the five dollars.

CHAPTER FOURTEEN

It was almost nine o'clock before John Peter Osgood heard that Ruby Lennox was dead. He heard it from the lieutenant, whose face was purple at the time.

"This tears it," the lieutenant said. "Curtis Rathjen or no Curtis Rathjen, this tears it wide open."

Ten minutes later Osgood was standing at the end of the garage where Ruby's body was still lying just as she'd fallen when the tire iron hit her on the head. In addition to Frenchy, the medical examiner, and a police photographer, the courtyard was crowded with gray-faced tenants who had just awakened to find murder in their back yard. No question about it this time. No tricky business with doped drinks and a hair dryer. Ruby Lennox was dead because someone had gone to a lot of trouble to make her that way.

"I found the body," Wallace Timm said. "I came around here to get the cans to take out front. Today is the day for picking up the empty cans."

Today was going to be the day for picking up more than empty cans, Osgood reflected. Two calls for the meat wagon within a week was quite a record for one small bungalow court. If this kept up, Curtis Rathjen would soon run out of tenants. With the exception of Timm, who probably got up with the birds, the remaining tenants had turned out in varying states of undress. Tony Carmen was wearing a very fancy brocade robe over his silk pajamas, and Sharl and Denise, who were more on the bargain-cotton side, had come out without their faces. But at the edge of the group was one tenant fully dressed in a crisp white uniform.

"Well, I see you're back again," Osgood said. "Have a pleasant week-end?"

Ann Jenner looked startled. She started to back away. "I'll be late for work," she murmured.

"Just a minute, Miss Jenner." Osgood shouldered his way past Tony and the girls to block her departure. "We'll have to question everybody here. You must realize that."

"You mean about—about *that?*"

Ann pointed toward Ruby's body and shuddered. "What else?" Osgood asked. "This isn't a Congressional investigating committee."

"But I don't know anything about it. I just came out when I heard the commotion."

"So did I," Tony said, and the girls chorused the same sentiment.

It was only what Osgood expected. If nobody knew anything about Jeri Lynn's supposedly accidental death they sure weren't going to volunteer anything about Ruby's definitely nonaccidental death. But there was a tire iron beside Ruby's body, and only two of the tenants owned automobiles. Frenchy brought up that matter when he returned from a quick inspection of the garage.

"There's only one car in there," he said, "an old sedan."

"That's my car," Ann said.

"Do you have a tire iron, Miss Jenner?"

The woman looked bewildered. "A tire iron?" she echoed.

"Yes, like the one that killed Ruby Lennox. Do you have one?"

Ann drew closer to the body and looked down at the blood-smeared weapon. "I suppose I do," she said weakly. "I really don't know for sure. I've never changed a tire."

"Well, I have," Tony volunteered, "and my tire iron's in the trunk of my car right now. I checked on it as soon as I saw what hit Ruby."

"Nice co-operation," Osgood murmured, and Tony, who was sort of an olive-green under all that sun tan, didn't seem to like his tone of voice.

"What do you mean by that, copper?" he demanded.

Osgood wasn't sure what he meant except that Tony was going to get a mouthful of knuckles if he called him copper like that again. Frenchy knew it, too. That's why he started talking so fast.

"About that tire iron," he said, "the reason I asked the nurse if she had one is because she doesn't have one now. I've looked in the trunk of her sedan and all I found was a beat-up spare and an old *Reader's Digest.*"

"But that doesn't mean anything!" Ann cried. "The trunk won't lock—the latch is broken. And nobody ever locks the garage!"

Osgood could believe that. The law required garage space for every rental, but Ann Jenner seemed to be the only tenant who used it for that purpose. It seemed to be a combination workshop, storage room, and catchall. Along with the boxes, trunks, and paint cans, there was a whole collection of both garden and carpenter tools in plain view. Ruby's killer had gone to a lot of trouble to find a weapon.

He eased off from the group around Ruby's body and took a look at her apartment. The door was unlocked and standing ajar, and inside the lights were burning. That seemed natural, because it was obvious that Ruby had been dead a good many hours. The place looked neat enough. Nothing upset or overturned. On one of the lamp tables he found a shot glass full of whisky that hadn't been touched. Whatever had drawn Ruby Lennox out in the darkness to meet a killer must have caught her between drinks, he reckoned, but it wouldn't do any harm to have the glass checked for prints. He was still nosing around in the apartment when Frenchy started yelling from outside. He answered the summons and found everybody standing around like a pack of hounds just catching the scent.

Frenchy was up on the roof deck. "The door's standing open and the cat's bawling in front of the refrigerator," he called down, "but there's no sign of the old girl."

For a moment only silence followed Frenchy's words, and then, from somewhere in that group of pale listeners, came two distinct gasps.

"Oh, no!" Denise cried. "That poor, dear soul! It couldn't be!"

Sharl just looked stricken, as if she were posing for a close-up at the rail of the sinking *Titanic*.

Later Osgood would learn what prompted this exhibition of dramatics, but at the moment he was too busy bounding up the stairs to join Frenchy. It was just as Frenchy said—the open door, the bawling cat, and one thing more. A trail of red ants making a raid on the top cupboard shelf led to the most interesting discovery of all: a cake with chocolate icing, pink sugar roses, and the greeting, *Happy Birthday Darling*.

It was torn, all right; it was shredded. A neurotic woman

with a talent for creating trouble had secreted a cake belonging to one dead woman and reacted to the death of another by chasing off in the night after a cat that wasn't lost. By the time Curtis Rathjen stumbled down to headquarters looking like a gray ghost with a nervous breakdown, every police officer in the city was getting a description of his sister as last seen by Denise and Sharl. If Wilma's brief appearance at the theater meant what it seemed to mean, Ruby must have died shortly before the eleven-o'clock curtain. No one but old man Timm, who claimed he'd gone to bed at nine-thirty, would admit to being on the premises at that hour, and it wasn't polite to ask such a question of Curtis Rathjen.

It wasn't necessary, either. Curtis was carrying a big grief, and the weight of it measured up to a couple of telephone calls he'd neglected to answer.

"Poor Wilma." He sighed. "I knew she wasn't well, but I never dreamed she could do a thing like this! If only I had called her last night, but it was so late when I got in!"

"In from where?" Osgood asked.

Curtis looked a little surprised, but no grief was private where murder was concerned, and so he related how he had taken a client to look at some property in Ventura County, wined and dined him, and hadn't reached home until almost midnight. There Mrs. Rathjen informed him that his sister had been trying to get in touch with him all evening.

"I thought surely she'd have gone to bed by that hour," he explained, "so I didn't call her."

"Did she tell your wife why she wanted to talk to you?"

Rathjen's faint smile looked pathetic. "Something about what she'd learned about one of the tenants," he said. "Wilma was always calling about that sort of thing. It's been only a few weeks since she wanted me to give Miss Lennox notice because she wouldn't lower her blinds at night."

"What about Jeri Lynn?" the lieutenant suggested. "Did your sister ever complain about her?"

"Jeri Lynn?" If Curtis got any more pale they'd have to bury him. "Great Scott!" he gasped. "Are you trying to tell me that my sister is responsible for her death, too?"

So far as Osgood was concerned nobody had to tell Curtis Rathjen anything; but this was the lieutenant's show now, and he gave him the whole spiel about the doped drink, the beauty-parlor appointment, and the small problem of how a girl who had just taken a knockout powder could kill herself. The way he told it made Osgood feel he'd never had a thing to do with the case, and he was beginning to wish he hadn't. Osgood was getting angry. Maybe it was because of all the questions he'd asked for nothing, or maybe because of the way Wilma had fooled him Saturday night with all that frank and honest talk until he'd gone away feeling sorry for this little woman with the frustrated life. He still did, and part of the reason for that was the way Curtis Rathjen was so quick to accept the obvious. Blood was supposed to be thicker than water, but Curtis seemed pretty anemic.

"Wasn't Miss Lynn a good friend of yours?" Osgood broke in, and everybody looked at him as if he'd just got in from Mars.

"A friend of mine?" Rathjen echoed. "Whatever gave you such an idea?"

"Oh, something I heard somewhere."

"From my sister, I'll warrant! What fantastic story did the woman tell you? Something about Miss Lynn not paying her rent?"

It was a good question. Osgood marveled that he hadn't thought of it himself.

"Didn't she?" he asked, and the red began to creep up on Rathjen's recently pale face.

"Of course she did!" he snapped. "When she was able. The poor girl suffered a breakdown some months ago, and so naturally she was a little in arrears. My sister wanted me to evict her, but I couldn't do that!"

"Why not?"

"When she was ill? Besides, I'd never collect the back rent that way."

It was a good thing Rathjen included the afterthought because someone might have remembered how pretty Jeri Lynn was. Someone besides Osgood. "Then you never let Miss Lynn drive your car?" he asked, and the balloon went up.

"Drive my car?" Rathjen howled. "Of course I didn't! Where did you ever get such a fantastic idea?"

Osgood looked at Frenchy, and Frenchy started sliding under the desk. There was such a thing as talking out of turn, and apparently Osgood had done it, because Curtis Rathjen had forgotten how grieved he was and was look- ing like an Eagle Scout accused of treason.

"Drive my car!" he repeated. "What did that poor woman tell you? And what kind of a police force is this, Lieutenant, when you have able-bodied men loitering around the office while my sister's at large? This man could recognize Wilma. Why isn't he out searching for her instead of asking these ridiculous questions?"

When a man like Curtis Rathjen put the matter that way, there wasn't much the lieutenant could do. "Please," he said, looking at Osgood, "go out and find something even if it's only a lost dog."

And so Osgood went out and found Phillip Blade.

It wasn't much of a feat. All he had to do was leave the lieutenant's office, elbow his way through the crowd of reporters that were waiting to get at Rathjen, and walk into a room where a couple of uniformed officers were looking pretty bored over the sad character they'd just picked up in a Hollywood bus station. With all that comb- ing of bars and cheap hotels, Phillip Blade would choose to sleep off his stupor in a place so public no one would notice another soldier. He looked pretty bad. His beard was a couple of days old, and his eyes looked like punctures in a dirty rug, but he managed a weak grin when he looked up and recognized Osgood.

"I heard you were looking for me," he said. "My bodyguard told me."

Twenty-four hours ago this find would have created quite a stir; but because Ruby Lennox, whose death made no sense at all, had been found with a tire-iron dent in her skull nobody was much interested in the soldier's lapse of memory.

"Did they tell you what I wanted you for?" Osgood asked.

The kid shrugged, and the exertion almost toppled him from his chair. "Nobody ever tells a soldier why," he said. " 'Ours not to reason why—'"

"Tuesday," Osgood broke in.

The word seemed to bring Blade out of the fog. "What's that?" he said.

"Tuesday morning your outfit hit the docks. Friday afternoon you came home to your wife. What kind of an army are they turning out these days?"

There was a nice, pear-shaped silence behind Osgood's query, and then Blade fished a pack of wilted cigarettes from his jacket pocket and tried to look nonchalant while getting a light from a book of matches that wouldn't hold still.

"I knew I should have told you about that," he muttered. "I would have if that cocky character in the bathing trunks hadn't made that crack about Jeri. But if you want to know where I was all that time, I was in a little hotel down near the harbor. I think I've got the name of it somewhere. I had a receipt for my room."

"For income-tax purposes?"

Blade ignored the innuendo. "For protection," he said.

"You've no idea how grateful the citizens can be for what a guy does for his country. They think nothing of charging twice for a room that's been paid up in advance, and I paid in advance so I could have a long, quiet rest with a couple of friendly bottles."

The soldier wasn't kidding about the receipt. He laid the cigarettes and matches down on the table and combed through his pockets until he found it. Osgood passed it on to a fellow officer who didn't need to be told to start checking. He didn't know why he was such a doubting Thomas, but that match book on the table might have had something to do with it.

"Then you were in that hotel until Friday," he mused, "with a beautiful wife waiting at home."

"That's just it—she wasn't waiting."

Blade took a couple of deep drags on his cigarette and then tried to meet Osgood's eyes. "No use lying about it," he muttered. "We were washed up. When I heard I was coming home, I wrote Jeri the good news. Right away she wrote back saying she wanted a divorce. She didn't say why, but I figured it was another guy."

So the kid wasn't fooled after all. Osgood felt a little better about the situation. He hated being cast as a sheep-herder. "Weren't you a little curious about that other guy?" he suggested.

Blade shook his head. "Why? When a thing's over it's over. One guy or another makes no difference. What chance does a marriage have when all you have is one week-end pass in over a year? I wrote Jeri that she could have the divorce if she still wanted it when I got back, and then I turned chicken when the ship docked, and couldn't face her. It took me until Friday to drink up enough courage. Then it was too late."

It seemed strange to hear a kid with all those ribbons on his tunic admit to being chicken, but not when his face was so near. A hang-over could make a man look that sick, but so could a lot of other things. Osgood had a couple of specific things in mind, but before he could ask any more questions, an outburst across the hall made the soldier swing around toward the door the departing officer had left half open.

"What's the riot?" he asked, and Osgood put it to him straight.

"Murder," he said.

"Is that right? Who was murdered?"

"A woman who lived just across the court from your wife."

It wasn't so much what Osgood said as what he didn't say that yanked Phillip Blade's attention back from that doorway. Murder was a tough thing to get used to even without a hang-over. Osgood watched him sweat awhile and then explained what had happened to Ruby Lennox when she went out in the darkness with her flashlight.

"Ruby Lennox," he repeated. "Did your wife ever mention that name in her letters?"

Blade shook his head. "I never heard it before," he said, "Who killed her?"

Practically any other man in the building would have answered that question without hesitation, but Osgood wasn't any other man. "We're hunting down a suspect," he said, "but nobody knows for sure. Now if only you hadn't been in that bus station last night, and had been strolling around the neighborhood at the right time—"

"Wait a minute. What are you driving at?"

"I'm not driving at anything; I'm just supposing. That's what happens when two beautiful women die at the same court in the same week. A man starts supposing."

It wasn't subtle, and Osgood didn't give a damn. Hero or no hero, this kid's thirst had given him a big headache, and he had an uneasy feeling that the big one was still to come. "But then you wouldn't remember, would you?" he added.

"No, I wouldn't! What's this got to do with me anyway?"

"Who said it had anything to do with you? I'm just trying to get a line on a murderer?"

"Well, don't expect me to help you. I can't even find where I left the top of my head."

Blade's boyish face was getting all twisted with anger again, and so Osgood decided to help him out. He picked up the match folder and read the cover blurb.

"Have you tried La Rene's Place?" he asked.

They might have had it out right then. They might have had a very heated but enlightening discussion, because Blade had lost his poise and Osgood was long out of patience. But just as they paused over that match folder, Frenchy bounced into the room with the story of a Hollywood bartender whose wife didn't like what he brought home instead of five dollars. To drown the commentary he'd switched on the radio and picked up a newscast that sent him chasing down to the police station with an opal ring in his hand.

"It's Wilma's ring," Frenchy said. "Brother Curtis identified it. Let's get started."

"Where?" Osgood asked, and Frenchy stared at him as if he had asparagus growing out of his head.

"Where do you think?" he howled. "We're going to comb the area. How far could the old girl get on five dollars?"

Wilma slept until almost noon. She had a cheap room with a lavatory, a metal bed, a dresser, and one window overlooking a parking lot. About eight o'clock the parking lot started filling up, and a little later the dancing school over the bus station started its first class of the day. But the autos, the busses, and even the dancing school couldn't arouse Wilma. She slept like the dead.

Then it was the resurrection. The noises came gradually,

as if moving in from a great distance, and the ceiling swam into focus with all its cracks and blisters and its old-fashioned light fixture that dropped downward like an accusing finger. Wilma sat upright, heart pounding, and tried to remember what had brought her to this strange place. And then she tried to forget. The red hair sat on the dresser top like a hennaed bird's nest. The green velvet coat sagged over the back of a straight wooden chair. The white fur piece looked like the ghost of something that had died across the foot of the bed. Now the waking nightmare returned, and she remembered that Ruby Lennox was dead because somebody wanted to kill Wilma Rathjen.

Somebody. The noises were more vivid now. Footsteps in the hall—voices and murmurings. Wilma crawled out of bed and dressed hurriedly as if any moment might bring a knock at the door from the hand of death. But the hall was empty when she went out, and she passed no one on the stairs. Downstairs was a small lobby where a collection of oddities—unshaven men in high-heeled boots and flabby-faced women in overaged finery—occupied the ancient lounges. She scrutinized them carefully from behind a potted plant, but none of them seemed interested in Wilma Rathjen. "When I worked with De Mille—" a cracked contralto voiced at her shoulder, but the words were for a Stetson-crowned giant who stroked his heavy mustache and gazed into the far pastures of the past. Now Wilma understood. She'd come straight to a nest of bit players and would-be actors—surely the last place anyone would expect to find Wilma Rathjen! For the first time since she'd started running there came a sense of sanctuary. These weird (and very likely wicked) creatures would hide her with themselves. She began to calculate how long the change from the five dollars would last, and how much she might get for the white fur. And then the street door opened and a uniformed policeman marched up to the desk.

"We're looking for an old dame, a loony," he said to the clerk. "Maybe you heard about her on the radio."

"The one that killed the blonde last night?"

"That's the one. We're checking all the hotels in this area. Seen anyone like this?"

Wilma edged back toward the stairway. She knew that it must be a photograph of herself that the policeman was showing to the clerk, and the only way he could have gotten a photograph was from Curtis. Then Curtis knew! Somehow she'd expected Curtis to take care of things. Even if he didn't believe her, he could fix it with the police. But now Curtis knew, and he hadn't fixed anything. A loony! She knew what that word meant. It meant there would be no chance to tell her story, and no one to listen if she tried. It meant that she wasn't safe even in this shabby hotel, and that she must find a back door before the policeman turned around.

There was a back door at the end of a passage behind the stairs. It opened into an alleyway that led into a street. Only the streets held any safety now.

CHAPTER FIFTEEN

It didn't seem such a big job to find one small, middle-aged woman with grayish-brown hair, no hat or coat, and no funds except five dollars. The bartender wasn't sure about the hair. "It looked red to me," he recollected, "but then the lights ain't so good at the bar. But I'd swear she was wearing some kind of white fur." His words made no sense at all until later in the day when a theft report came in from that little theater. By that time Wilma was on a streetcar bound for downtown and Osgood was getting thoroughly discouraged.

It wasn't the needle-in-the-haystack search; it was the evidence piling up against the fugitive. Evidence should make a policeman happy but not when it was against his every instinct. Back at headquarters, in a day growing dank with fog, he went over the report on the fingerprints taken from that glass in Ruby's apartment and scowled.

"Wilma Rathjen drinking whisky?" he marveled. "That doesn't sound right somehow."

"There's your motive," Frenchy said. "She killed Ruby because the gal was trying to corrupt her with liquor."

It wasn't as farfetched as it sounded. The routine check they'd run on Ruby Lennox bore out Frenchy's original claim that he remembered the blonde from somewhere. It was quite a few somewheres that she'd gone afoul of the law by working on the wrong side of the bar, and it all stacked up to a certain validity in Wilma's complaint against unlowered blinds.

"The hand of God," Frenchy muttered. "There's the cause of most of the trouble in the world. Some crackpot gets the idea he has a mandate from heaven to eliminate sinners, and the first thing you know the blood is ankle-deep."

"What about Jeri Lynn?" Osgood protested. "I suppose Wilma Rathjen doped her drink, carried her to the tub, and then tossed in that hair dryer all by herself."

"Why not? I've known screwballs to have the strength of Goliath."

There was no use arguing with Frenchy or the evidence. There were no fingerprints on the tire iron, but Wilma's fingerprints were on the whisky glass, Jeri Lynn's long-missing cake was on her cupboard shelf, and flight was the last resort of the guilty. But what about all the other sprinters on this team? Osgood paused to consider his own unspoken question, and it seemed that the starting gun had sounded early. First, it was Ann Jenner in a deception that still hadn't been explained; then Phillip Blade's big thirst that had taken him so far from that plush hotel, and then old man Timm's Saturday-night excursion that had not only sealed his eye but his lips as well. Recalling Saturday night brought back the picture of Wilma Rathjen calmly confessing her foreknowledge of Jeri Lynn's death— but was that all she'd confessed? "I make mistakes," she'd said. "Sometimes I order things and the customers never come—" Ringing up a fake sale and taking that cake home was just the kind of foolish thing a fear-crazed woman might do, and fear alone was no proof of guilt. If it were, Jeri Lynn must have been murdered by a gang!

But Frenchy had X-ray eyes. "I don't get it," he said, spoiling a perfectly good meditation. "I've never seen you so hard to convince. What is this with you and the old girl?"

That was one question Osgood wouldn't have answered even if he could, but he did know that the search for Wilma Rathjen would go on from here without him. Maybe she was as guilty as the evidence indicated. Maybe she was crazy enough to keep in a cage and he wasn't far behind, but some of those questions would have to be answered before he could be sure. Even a crazy woman deserved that much of a chance.

Saturday morning Osgood had started out to interview one Arnold Fergus, M.D., only to be sidetracked on a futile search for Phillip Blade. Now that Blade had come back like a good boy when nobody wanted him any more, the doctor's office seemed a good place to start picking up old broken threads. It was getting late by the time he pulled into the small parking lot behind the medical center, and it looked as if business was just about over for the day. He recognized Ann Jenner's old jalopy nosed in along-side a couple of inconspicuous coupes, but the belle of the parking area was a big Cadillac sedan with Fergus's name on the registration slip. Osgood wasn't envious, but he was a little sensitive about Cadillacs after Frenchy started relaying beauty-shop gossip. There was no lien holder on that registration slip, either. It was nice to know the young doctor was doing so well.

But the waiting-room was empty when Osgood got inside, and nobody sat at the reception desk. He went straight to the door of the inner office and then hesitated at the sound of voices on the other side.

"I'm afraid I haven't been much good today," Ann Jenner's voice was saying. "Arnold, what am I going to do?"

There was a note of desperation in the nurse's voice that caused Osgood to freeze with his hand on the doorknob. It seemed a shame to spoil this little after-hours conversation.

"Why do anything?" the doctor answered. "You've stuck it out this long."

"I've hidden out, you mean! When I think of that poor woman—"

"Then don't think of her! The police will find her unless she's destroyed herself, and there isn't much chance of that. I imagine she thinks pretty highly of herself even if the rest of us are a bunch of sinners."

They were strong words, but the doctor didn't seem able to convince either the nurse or himself. After a little silence he voiced an almost plaintive: "What do you want to do?"

"I don't know," she said. "Sometimes I think it would be best to go to the police with the whole story. They won't stop with an investigation of Ruby's death—not when they're already suspicious. If you'd seen the way Sergeant Osgood looked at me this morning—"

Ann Jenner's voice stopped abruptly. The trouble with hanging onto a doorknob during an interesting conversation was that it was apt to start turning and attract unwanted attention. Osgood's listening game was over the instant Fergus jerked open the door.

"Sorry I didn't make an appointment," Osgood said, "but then you were supposed to call me—remember?"

He could have made an omelet out of all that egg on everybody's face. For just a moment the doctor seemed inclined to shove him back through the door and slam it, but Osgood weighed too much with that badge in his pocket, and Ann Jenner talked too much after office hours.

"Now, what is this story Miss Jenner has for the police?" Osgood added, and the white flag went up like a rocket.

The story Osgood heard, and later relayed to headquarters with more than a twinge of regret, had to do with a Good Samaritan who overdid it, at least, that's how it sounded when the nurse stood up as tall as she could in her rubber-soled Oxfords and began reciting like an honor student. "It's all my fault," she insisted. "Doctor Fergus was only trying to protect me when he lied to you Saturday."

"From what?" Osgood asked.

"From suspicion. He could tell from your questions that you knew Jeri had been drugged before her death. I knew all along because I drugged her."

It was the kind of confession that usually came after hours of grilling and maybe a little exercise, and the simpleness of it threw Osgood off guard. Maybe the girl had meant what she said about going to the police. Maybe if he kept his mouth shut he'd learn why.

"It was Tuesday," she continued, "the day Jeri died. I didn't get away from the office until almost six-thirty. The doctor had some important X rays coming in and I stayed to receive them. Driving out of the lot I saw Jeri just leaving the beauty shop across the street, so I called to her and we drove home together. I wanted to have a talk with her anyway."

Dr. Fergus cleared his throat, and the nurse hesitated. For the first time her eyes sought the floor.

"What about?" Osgood prodded.

"About her health," she said. "It wasn't good, you know. She was just getting over one breakdown from trying to burn the candle at both ends and seemed headed for another. Living so close by, I could see what was happening. I tried to talk her into staying in just one night to get some sleep."

"And she told you to mind your own business because she had a heavy date."

Ann Jenner's head came up quickly. "How did you know?" she asked.

"From her beauty operator. You don't happen to know the identity of that date, do you?"

It might have been relief that brought the color back to Ann's face, or maybe she was just getting warm. "No, I don't," she said. "Jeri never confided in me. But I did urge her to call it off. She looked exhausted and complained of a headache—she suffered from migraine, you know. Well, the short of it was that I promised to bring over something for her headache as soon as I put the car away and I did. I brought two sleeping pills."

"The Scotch was Jeri's," Ann added before Osgood could ask. "Her standard cure-all. A fresh drink was all poured out and waiting on the desk when I reached the apartment. Jeri was in the bedroom using the phone and I heard her say she couldn't talk any more because she had to meet someone for dinner. The water was running for her bath, and it was useless to argue so I just dropped the pills in her glass before she came back. After that I sat around and talked until she went to sleep on the divan. That's how I left her—sleeping on the divan."

The girl's voice trailed off into silence. She sagged back against the desk with a forlorn look adding unearned years to her face, and Dr. Fergus placed an encouraging hand on her shoulder. It was all very sincere and very disturbing if true.

"The apartment was unlocked when you left it, I suppose," Osgood said.

Ann nodded wearily. "I never thought to release the latch—"

"And Jeri's heavy date was on his way—"

"Oh, no. She was meeting him. She usually went out to meet her dates. I guess she was ashamed of her shabby apartment."

Osgood frowned. There could be another reason, but this was no time to trouble the waters. And that still didn't explain why the disappointed dinner date didn't check up on his missing girl friend. There was such a thing as curiosity. For instance, a policeman could be curious as to why this overconscientious nurse hadn't checked back on her patient, and why she'd kept her story secret so long. And such curiosity could spoil the good manners of a prominent physician who disliked policemen and publicity.

"Great Scott, man," Fergus protested, "my nurse is a busy woman! I doubt if she gave the girl another thought until her death was announced. What purpose would her story have accomplished then? The death was accidental."

"Even with sleeping pills?"

"Why not? Miss Lynn may have revived just enough to stumble-back into that bathroom and kill herself—that's what Ann thinks. That's why she's been so upset that I had to take her to my mother's place on the desert to calm down. We returned late last night and then this morning—"

The doctor needed no more words. This morning Ruby Lennox had been found dead and Wilma Rathjen was missing. It was amazing how the souls were being bared in the wake of these twin events—first Phillip Blade and his broken marriage and now Ann Jenner and her eleventh-hour conscience. Osgood didn't like to be cynical, but he couldn't help realizing how the nurse's story could remove Jeri's death from the doubtful column. It could be written off as an accident the way the doctor told it, or added to Wilma's account. The girl had been left in a helpless condition, and the time was right. It was right for Ruby's six-thirty memory and it still left plenty of time for the nurse to put away her car, return to her apartment, and then get Jeri off to sleep before Wilma came home.

"As a matter of fact," Ann reflected. "I think I saw her coming down the street as I drove off with Doctor Fergus—That was later when he came for the X rays. We went out on a call?'

For a man who'd just found the first genuine break in two puzzling deaths, Osgood felt miserable.

"I don't suppose either of you went back to look for that glass after the body was found," he suggested.

A pair of blank stares gave eloquent reply. He'd have to look farther for Wilma's prowlers, and that left only one question for these suddenly helpful people—a question that made the doctor's eyeglasses bounce with surprise.

"My birthday?" he echoed. "It's in November. Why?"

"I'll send you a card," Osgood muttered, and stalked out into a dripping dusk.

The white fur smelled like a wet dog in the rain. It wasn't really rain; it was more of a penetrating mist, but Wilma was chilled through. The green velvet coat was no protection against such weather, and her feet felt like buckets of ice, but she had to keep walking. That was the important thing, to keep in motion so nobody would notice her and remember a picture that now decorated every front page.

It seemed that she'd been walking forever. While the stores were still open, she'd found shelter among the main-floor shoppers, but soon the stores closed, the offices emptied, and the streets began to look lonely. To be alone was to be conspicuous and so Wilma sought out the peopled places. The streets turned shabby. Windows of expensively draped mannequins were replaced by credit clothiers, one flight up; wide-faced movie palaces shrank to narrow tunnels with gaudy pictures of undressed girls in their lobbies, and chrome-front restaurants gave way to cheap cafeterias with the menu pasted in the window. Now Wilma wasn't alone any more. It was as if the city had tilted and everything that wasn't fastened down had tumbled into one bright artery filled with noise, neons, and a strange and terrible people. There were painted women, beggars and fops, shadows that moved and shadows that didn't, and through this alien and evil-smelling world Wilma walked like an exile praying for a miracle. Nothing else could penetrate this Sodom and Gomorrah with traffic lights.

It was a traffic light that got her into trouble. A misstep on the slippery sidewalk sent her stumbling against one of the shadows that moved and a hand reached out to steady her. "Don't touch me!" Wilma cried out, and the shadow with the hand laughed.

"Look, sister, if you can't carry it don't take on such a load," the shadow said.

It was a foreign language to Wilma, but merely to be addressed by one of these terrible creatures was enough to bring on a minor panic. Breaking loose from the pressure on her arm, she started to run—heedless of warning shouts, heedless of traffic signals, honking horns, or the outraged whistle of the traffic officer. From the opposite curb she looked back for some sign of her molester only to face the oncoming figure of the last thing on earth she cared to encounter—a policeman! Wilma ran. Just around the corner was a store with an open doorway and some people gathered inside. She joined them and moments later found herself standing in line with a tray in her hands.

She'd fled into one of the cheap cafeterias, and now that she thought of it—and smelled the aroma of hot coffee from the tall chrome containers—Wilma knew that she must have nourishment. She must be careful, of course. The change from the bartender's five dollars was all she had, or was likely to have for some time, but the coffee was hot and the doughnuts were cheap.

A hard-faced woman with orange-tinted hair shoved her tray into Wilma's back while she took the money out of a knotted handkerchief. Counting the change like a miser, she paid the cashier and then found a table where she could keep her eyes on the door. That policeman had given up the chase, but there were other policemen.

"Lousy weather, ain't it, honey?"

An unexpected voice in her ear was enough to make Wilma tremble even when she wasn't a fugitive. She started to rise but the way was blocked by the orange haired woman seated beside her. "Hope you don't mind company," the woman said, with a toothy smile. "Just between you and me, there's a man across the aisle who's been tailin' me. I figured if I sat with somebody he'd go away."

Wilma shuddered. There was a man across the aisle, obviously indifferent to anything but his plate, and seemed quite unlikely that he, or anyone, could do any damage to this derelict. She smelled of whisky and dirt and cheap face powder. Any appetite Wilma had was gone now.

"Go away!" Wilma cried. "There are plenty of tables! Leave me alone!"

The woman's bloodshot eyes narrowed to the point of disappearance and then her heavy lips parted in a twisted smile. "No offense, dearie," she muttered. "I didn't know you was so antisocial." She left the table without further comment, didn't even take her tray along, but Wilma couldn't stop trembling. It was a time when everything seemed to give way at once: body, nerves, and heart. *What am I doing in this terrible place?* she wondered. *What am I doing among these terrible people?* She looked down at the two stale doughnuts on her plate. No reputable establishment would handle such stock. It was day-old! Waggoner never tolerated day-old!

Wilma began to weep. Now it seemed that she would

never see her home again, her beautiful little apartment, her store—why, even Waggoner could be nice at times! Her hand groped inside the pocket of the green velvet coat for a handkerchief and came back empty. She stared at the empty hand, searched the pocket again, searched the floor. Then Wilma looked up in time to see the woman with the orange hair disappearing through the street door, and all the lights came on at once.

Forty-three years of repression fell in the clatter of Wilma's abandoned chair. A lady didn't scream, "Stop, thief," and chase after an ancient of the streets for the paltry prize of a few dollars in a knotted handkerchief; but then a lady didn't know hunger and fear. Laughter and jeers didn't matter now. The moving shadows pushed against her, and Wilma pushed back, because now only one object in the world had any importance—a wicked thief with orange hair. The woman ran into a dark doorway and Wilma ran after her. It was like invading oblivion until her eyes adjusted to the dim lights and her ears to the beat of a jukebox lament.

A couple of hippy women sat at the bar with some baby-faced sailors, but the women were much too young. Across the room was a row of booths, and this time Wilma wasn't afraid to look, but nobody in the booths had orange hair. Whirling about, Wilma contacted a waiter-borne tray with disastrous results to the refreshments, but even a deluge of liquor couldn't stop her now. At the rear of the room a pair of dirty drapes swayed like a beckoning finger. Ignoring the protests about her, she ran forward into a narrow hall where one naked bulb dangled from the ceiling and two painted doors advertised the facilities of the house.

The light in the ladies' room seemed to have burned out. Wilma held open the door to catch the illumination from the hall, and that was when she saw her thief. The fiery hair, the drooping lips and cruel eyes—all the ugly evilness of her was crouched and waiting just inside that shadowy room. Wilma lunged forward, and so did her prey. They met in a shattering, splintering crash....

It didn't take long for the police to come. This particular bar supplied some of their very best customers, but the place had quieted down by the time they arrived. The drunk who'd tried to wreck the place was cornered in one of the booths and only the unhappy owner was making any noise.

"Twenty bucks!" he bawled, over and over again. "Twenty bucks I paid for a mirror in the powder room just to give the place class—and this loony has to smash it with her fists! I ask you, how much can a dame hate herself?"

CHAPTER SIXTEEN

It was a long time before Curtis came. It was a long time before anybody knew enough to call him. There was nothing to distinguish Wilma from all the other female drunks taking the city's overnight cure. The tousled hair, the glassy eyes, the stench of liquor on her clothing—these were standard requirements for enrollment, and Wilma didn't protest. A kind of numb terror had come over her, and her tongue was too thick for speech. Whatever happened now she would submit in silence. The crowded cell, the raving, tittering women of every age and description, the muscular matrons and the clanging door—all of these things she saw as if from a great distance. The world had gone mad, and Wilma Rathjen could do nothing to stop it. There were no miracles after all.

But she had lost the red wig in the police car, and when one of the arresting officers discovered it he had a good laugh with his partner—there was no limit to what these queers would wear—and then got to thinking about an all-points bulletin on the woman wanted for that Hollywood killing. Back at city jail they made a fast run-down on Wilma's apparel: green velvet coat, white fur matted with liquor and stained with blood from her lacerated hands, green satin pumps with the heels half broken off—It was then that the wires started humming.

Half an hour later the matron came to get Wilma out of the cell. She had to find her first. Somebody had tacked up a small mirror on the far wall, and that's where Wilma had gone. She stood transfixed, studying her image as if it were the portrait of some unfamiliar face that she must memorize. But she didn't resist the tug on her arm. In the cell, out of the cell, it was all the same now.

They walked down a long corridor and into a bright room where Curtis stood among a group of police officers like a schoolboy called before the principal for reprimand. "Good Lord," he gasped, at the sight of her, "it is my sister! I was sure there must be some mistake."

At least one of the officers present knew exactly what Curtis meant. Twenty minutes ago Osgood had been questioning the landlady of a cheap rooming house just off Hollywood Boulevard. Ann Jenner's story had caused quite a flurry of excitement with the powers that be, but it was the report of a rifled wardrobe that had put him back on the search for Wilma. That was the act of a desperate woman. She couldn't be running that hard just for exercise.

But even an up-to-date description failed to bring any trace of the woman. He'd come back to the sedan and started telling Frenchy about an idea he had for checking the gospel missions when the radio came on with an announcement that Wilma Rathjen had been picked up in a downtown barroom brawl and was in the drunk tank. It was like hearing that Alcoholics Anonymous was throwing a cocktail party. A thing like that had to be seen to be believed, and Frenchy had the siren going all the way in.

When Wilma walked into the room, Osgood felt sick. He'd seen women in the same condition thousands of times, but not this woman. Not a woman so fastidious in her dress and conduct, and so pitifully proud of her furniture and her chocolate cups. In the forty-eight hours since he'd seen her last, the woman seemed to have matriculated from hell. Her face was a washed-out gray, and her staring eyes didn't seem to be able to focus. She faced Curtis without a sign of recognition, and he stared back as if looking at a ghost.

"Wilma, where have you been? What have you done?"

The questions were spontaneous, and yet it seemed that there should have been something more for a brother to say to his sister at that moment. At least, it seemed that way to Osgood. What Wilma thought wasn't discernible through her silence. Even her face seemed frozen.

"She won't answer," the matron advised coolly, "She just stands and stares at a mirror."

"Better keep her away from it," cautioned one of the officers. "That's how she got in here—breaking a mirror."

"I don't understand," Curtis said weakly. "Wilma's not like that at all. Do you understand, Doctor Lindsey?"

Curtis hadn't come to this ordeal alone. Two men in dark suits and Homburgs tagged at his heels like a couple of left-over pallbearers in search of a funeral. One had the look of a lawyer anticipating an interesting fee, and the other responded to Curtis's question by stepping forward and peering at Wilma as if she were a specimen on a miscroscopic slide. At the sight of him she gave the first sign of recognition. She shrank back against the wall.

"She's obviously in a state of shock," the doctor observed. "What are those lacerations on her hands?"

"I told you," the officer said. "She smashed a mirror."

The doctor nodded gravely. "Self-mutilation. I was afraid

something like this might develop. I warned you, Mr. Rathjen, if you remember."

"But you said if she kept active—"

Curtis broke off his protest in embarrassed silence. It was obvious to everybody how active Wilma had been lately, and it was also obvious that she couldn't go back to that drunk tank. Now everybody began to talk at once—Curtis, the lawyer, the police, and even Dr. Lindsey. "This woman needs immediate attention," he insisted. "I'll not take the responsibility for the consequences if she's withheld from treatment any longer."

But the officer in charge wasn't impressed.

"You don't have to take the consequences. We've handled psychos before."

"But I'm Miss Rathjen's doctor. I know her case history!"

"The only case we're interested in is a simple case of murder."

A flicker of interest lighted Wilma's staring eyes. Murder. Osgood, who kept his mouth shut in the presence of so much brass, could almost see her trembling lips form the word. Her eyes swept the room quickly, and she seemed to be standing on tiptoe.

"It's not going to do any good to question the woman in her present state," the doctor said firmly. "The situation clearly calls for psychotherapy. It may require shock treatment or even hypnosis to get a coherent statement from her. Look for yourselves. Is this woman in any condition to make a responsible confession?"

With all that oratory, everybody but Osgood had momentarily forgotten Wilma. Suddenly she was the focal point for all eyes, and it was like turning on a spotlight. Nobody seemed to breathe until the doctor reached out his hand.

"No!" Wilma screamed. "Don't come near me!"

Her first words, and they came like the crashing of cymbals. Lindsey drew back. It was impossible not to draw back in the face of that delivery. Wilma stood alone, pressed against the wall with her arms spread out like a living cross. The doctor recovered first.

"No one is going to hurt you, Miss Rathjen," he said. "We only want to help you."

"That's not true!"

"But of course it's true! You remember me, don't you? And surely you remember your own brother?"

Wilma didn't seem to be listening. Her eyes made a frantic sweep of the room. The matron blocked the hall door, and at least six men stood between her and the only other exit. Even so, Osgood could almost feel her muscles tighten for the try. She'd never make it. She'd never get away again. A kind of helpless pity caught at his throat, and then, across that room of anxious faces, she saw him. Her eyes stopped searching and fastened on him like a lost child at last catching sight of one familiar face.

"Don't let them take me!" she cried out. "Don't let them kill me!"

It was like a plea from the bottom of hell. Osgood's palms were suddenly wet.

"Who wants to kill you?" he demanded.

"No one wants to kill her," Curtis said crossly. "It's a complex, isn't it, Doctor? It's a persecution complex."

"Shut up!" Osgood snapped. "I asked your sister, not you! Who wants to kill you, Miss Rathjen?"

Something had happened in the room. Men who hadn't even been aware of Osgood's presence stepped aside, or were swept aside as he came toward Wilma. For a few moments there were just the two of them in the entire world.

"I—I don't know," she answered. "The faces."

"What faces?"

"All of the faces. Can't you see? All of the faces are evil, even my own!"

"This is nonsense," Curtis broke in. "Doctor Lindsey is right. My sister is in no condition to be questioned."

"Why not? Haven't you had time to have her brain washed?"

It was Osgood's own words that brought him back to reality. That was no way to speak to Curtis Rathjen and his expensive protectors. He was making an everlasting fool of himself over a crazy woman, with blood on her hands; but he couldn't help himself. Even a crazy woman should have a chance to speak for herself. How else could anyone tell the sane from the insane?

But the situation was getting out of hand, and so Dr. Lindsey took charge. There must be a quieter room where he could look after the poor woman until it was decided what was to be done with her. Some private room with a cot.

"No! I don't want to go with you!" Wilma cried. Suddenly she was wrapped around Osgood's neck. Her thin arms clutching him, clawing him, clinging to him like one about to drown. And then stronger arms were tearing her away.

"I don't want to go! I want to go home! Please, I want to go home!"

She was still screaming as they carried her back down the hall, and Osgood, who couldn't understand why, stood like the core of a man with his insides ripped out.

He couldn't get it out of his mind. This was no kind of a job for a man with a spine made of jelly, and God knows he'd seen enough grief of all sizes in the past nineteen years so that one more life down the drain shouldn't make any difference. But it did. Something Osgood couldn't define made all the difference in the world. He expected to hear about it from Frenchy, but the drive back to Hollywood was strangely silent. The routine calls on the radio made periodic breaks in the silence until

Frenchy shut the darned thing off. The special detail out on search for Wilma Rathjen could go home now. It was all over except for the shouting of tomorrow morning's headlines.

And it was almost tomorrow morning. The streets were empty and dark now, except for an occasional all-night gas station or hash house, and at this hour a late celebrant had to know where to go for a nightcap. Frenchy knew exactly where to go. He had the sedan nosed into La Rene's parking lot and the motor cut before Osgood realized where they were.

"Come on," Frenchy said. "As of now we're off duty, and I'm buying you a drink."

"I don't drink," Osgood muttered.

"Tonight you do. Your nerves are tighter than a matron's girdle. Something's got to give."

Any other time Osgood would have put up an argument, but tonight he was halfway inclined to think Frenchy was right about a lot of things. They went inside and walked over to the bar. Nobody's business could flourish all the time, and tonight La Rene's Place looked as if the receivers were just around the corner. It was the Monday-night slump with the last show over and the chairs already stacked up against the tables. There were only two customers at the bar, and since one of them was Matt Flavin, it didn't look as if La Rene figured to break even.

Frenchy ordered a pair of Scotches and started squinting about the dark room. With stained-glass windows it would have made a dandy mortuary.

"What's the matter with the jukebox?" he asked. "Are there union hours for it, too?"

Nobody answered, but the customer who wasn't Matt got up from a stool at the far end of the bar and came over to join the new arrivals. The customer was Tony Carmen. Osgood hardly recognized him with clothes on.

"Catch the old girl yet?" he queried.

"Get lost!" Frenchy said.

"What's the matter? Such smart cops and they can't even find one crazy dame!"

Tony had a glass of amber liquid in one hand and, from the looks of him, a lot more glasses inside. Bottled courage seemed to put a big chip on his beefy shoulders, and this was no time to have one of Osgood's pet annoyances hanging around. Frenchy had worked with him long enough to know what swaggering kids did to his blood pressure.

"Why don't you go home, sonny?" he suggested. "Maybe you have to get up in the morning for something—going to work, for instance."

"Who works?" Tony sneered.

"Most of the people who like to eat regularly."

"Suckers!" Tony drained his glass and slapped it back on the bar top. "What kind of work do you think I could get, anyway? Delivering papers, maybe? Any day now Uncle's going to send Tony one of those cheerful little greetings that says I've got a steady job with all expenses paid, including a funeral if it so happens I should need one. Who gives a decent job to a ripe One A?"

All this time Matt Flavin sat like a happy Buddha contemplating the brimming glass before him. Now he swung around and grabbed Tony's shoulder with a fatherly hand. "Are you going into the army, son?" he asked. "Why didn't you say so before? George, give this young man a drink on the house. Give him anything he wants."

"There, you see? You're a hero already," Frenchy said.

Tony grinned crookedly. "Sure, me and Phillip Blade. Too bad I wasn't in uniform a long time ago. Maybe Jeri would have married me instead of that chump."

Osgood hadn't been paying much attention to the small talk going on at his elbow, but when Tony tossed out Jeri's name that way it pulled his mind back from that grim scene at the city jail and stirred up a tug of curiosity.

Jeri didn't seem the type to fall for a guy in uniform. He gave the thought a voice, and Tony almost fell off the bar stool laughing.

"Not old Jeri!" he howled. "With her it wasn't the uniform; it was the insurance policy that went with it. Then Blade had to double-cross her and not get killed after all. Rotten luck!"

"A fine lad, Blade," Matt murmured sleepily. "A very fine lad."

It was an observation that took a few seconds to soak in. Osgood had been so interested in the falling embers from Tony's torch that he almost missed the significance of Matt's words. And then it all came back to him. A couple of millenniums ago, when the day was in the morning, Phillip Blade had strolled into the station to see what all the shouting was about. He'd smoked a cigarette and left a match folder on the desk that was a lot more informative than that vague story of a lost week-end. All of this came back to mind now, and with it a twinge of excitement that was arriving just a little late in the game.

"Did you know Phillip Blade?" he demanded.

Matt smiled reminiscently. "It was here in our little club that he first met our Jeri. Their romance blossomed under this very roof."

"Romance!" Tony snorted, but Matt took no note of the interruption.

"Of course, I didn't know they were married," he added. "The little vixen didn't tell old Matt about that."

The excitement was getting stronger. Maybe the whisky had something to do with it. "Have you seen him since he came home?" he asked, and Matt nodded happily. "Sure, I've seen him. I saw him just the other night."

"What night?"

"Look, Johnny," Frenchy broke in, "what's the point of getting steamed up again? Relax. I'll buy you another drink." But Osgood brushed him aside and repeated the question. He had to wait for an answer until Matt, obeying an immediate impulse at the suggestion of a drink, drained his own glass. But it was an answer worth waiting for.

"Saturday," Matt said, wiping his mouth with a silk pocket handkerchief. "It must have been Saturday because the poor lad had such a time getting anyone's attention in the crowd. He was awfully upset."

"What about?"

"About what happened to Dick Tracy in the Sunday comics!"

Matt's voice couldn't have changed that much. Osgood swung around and found La Rene standing where the bartender had been. Just when he'd cornered someone who wasn't tongue-tied, the vigilantes had to come along and ring curfew. But Matt was too liquored up to pay any attention to the dark warning in La Rene's eyes. "No, sweetie," he protested, "the boy was asking about Jeri, don't you remember? He wanted to know what company she'd been keeping while he was away."

"Now that's a coincidence," Osgood said. "It so happens that I'm interested in the same subject. What did you tell him, Matt?"

"What could he tell him?" La Rene snapped. "I told you the last time you came snooping around that Jeri hadn't been in since I tied a can to her tail."

"The last time I came here was Saturday night. You never said a word about Blade being here."

"He wasn't. He'd already gone."

"Just the same, you might have mentioned it. You knew the whole force was alerted for him."

La Rene was getting up quite a sweat in spite of the chilly turn of the weather. Just to look at her was a lot more warming than the whisky Frenchy kept shoving at him. "I'm not on the police force," she retorted, "and I'm not getting mixed up in messes that don't concern me. If Jeri was playing around, and she probably was, Matt and

I don't know a damned thing about it! Now finish your drink and get out of here. I don't like cops hanging around my place!"

Osgood finished his drink like a good boy, but it didn't change anything. He still wanted to ask questions. "How do you like your landlord?" he asked. "Does he turn any screws?"

"What do you mean by a crack like that?"

"What could I mean? After all, what's wrong with a beautiful girl getting her apartment rent-free when she's too sick to work for her keep?"

"Sick!" Tony exploded. "That little schemer was never sick a day of her life unless it was from a hang-over."

There was no getting around it, this cure of Frenchy's was amazing. Ten minutes ago Osgood had been ready to throw in the sponge and himself along with it; but now, with just a couple of drinks under his belt, he was hearing the most interesting things. He turned around and stared at Tony. What a pleasure it would be to re-arrange his pretty face.

"Now it's your turn," he said quietly. "What do you mean by a crack like that?"

"You figure it out," Tony muttered. "You're the smart cop."

But John Peter Osgood wasn't a smart cop at all. He was just a big, blundering bull of a cop with a lump of grief inside him that had to explode somewhere. Curtis Rathjen could shove him around, La Rene could order him out of the club, but this punk kid had gone too far! Frenchy sensed what was coming and bellowed a protest, but Frenchy was just a noise at his shoulder. A fist the size of a picnic ham smacked into Tony's face, and the mate to it plowed into his middle like a bulldozer gouging out real estate. Tony crumpled like an empty sack, and it was a delicious feeling to watch him drop. Osgood wanted to go on pounding until the kid didn't have a face, but

Frenchy was dragging on his arm, and La Rene was screaming like a banshee.

"Not in here! I don't want any rough stuff in my place!"

Poor La Rene, it might cost extra to have the porter mop up the blood. Instead of hitting Tony again, Osgood yanked him up against the bar and made a quick search of his pockets. Oh, to have found something on him, a gun, a reefer, or a needle! But Tony was clean except for a crumpled racing form and an expensive leather wallet.

"Leave him alone," Frenchy coaxed. "Come on, let's get out of here."

But first Osgood had to look at the driver's license. In the little square where it called for the date of birth he read: *August 8, 1934.* Sadly, he shoved the wallet back into Tony's pocket and let him fall. This was no birthday-cake boy.

Outside in the parking lot Frenchy sounded off. "That's the last time I buy you a drink," he said. "You're liable to kill somebody someday. And wait until the lieutenant hears about this!"

Osgood didn't give a damn for the lieutenant. It was a stinking job anyway. All he ever came in contact with was dirt and filth. He looked up at the enticing smiles on La Rene's billboard, and it came to him that the whole world was just a big floor show of dirt and filth with the score played by an orchestra of cash registers. What was that crazy thing Wilma Rathjen had yelled about the evil faces? It didn't sound so crazy now, and it was a fine world when the loonies made more sense than the normal people.

"To hell with the lieutenant!" he muttered. "I never wanted to be a cop anyway. I only got this lousy badge because the old man was killed and I wanted to square things. But what's the use? Nobody can ever square things."

For once Frenchy didn't argue. "That's what I've been trying to tell you. You've got to live and let live."

"Live! You call this living? I'm all through. I'm turning my badge before they drag me screaming and yelling down some hall. Tomorrow. First thing tomorrow."

"Sure," Frenchy said, "Tomorrow."

CHAPTER SEVENTEEN

Osgood was up early in the morning. He hadn't done much sleeping—Frenchy's cure didn't work on everybody—but he'd done a lot of thinking, and sometimes that was the only cure. It was almost dawn when he reached a decision. Maybe he couldn't square the whole world, but he could at least square himself. Living was a private enterprise anyway; a man could break his neck trying to see which way the crowd went.

And so Osgood was up early with the day mapped out ahead of him like a secret mission. After breakfast he made a phone call that told him Wilma Rathjen was still out from that sedative she'd been given, and the rest of the interested parties had all gone home. One of those homes had a very impressive address...

Curtis Rathjen lived in a neighborhood where everybody had three television sets: one for the children, one for the servants, and one to entertain the internal-revenue man while the owner called a lawyer. The house had a Mediterranean influence, and the butler resembled the Rock of Gibraltar until Osgood flashed his badge. After that, he was shown into a breakfast nook the size of a small ballroom, where Curtis Rathjen was sipping his chilled grapefruit juice. Curtis looked terrible. His fancy brocade dressing gown was wasted effort, because nothing could compete with the desolation in his eyes. He asked about

Wilma, and Osgood helped himself to a chair before answering. That left one less object for Curtis to throw if his blood pressure rose.

The report on Wilma only added to Curtis's anxiety. A policeman for breakfast wasn't on the usual bill of fare, but before he could protest Osgood took the floor.

"Mr. Rathjen," he asked, "do you really think your sister killed Ruby Lennox?"

It was a query that caught Curtis with his jaw down. "What—what else is there to think?" he stammered. "She did run away—"

"People do sometimes. Sometimes they even get so crazy with fear they run right into the thing they're trying to escape."

"But fear of what? What did my sister have to fear?"

It was Curtis who asked the crazy questions now. What did anyone have to fear?

"She told us last night," Osgood said. "Death."

Osgood didn't know if the idea was new to Curtis Rathjen, or if his face had taken on shock as a permanent expression. He started to protest again, but now he was getting too interested to interrupt. Osgood had a theory. It wasn't brand new—it must have been knocking around in the back of his mind for a couple of days—but it took Wilma's terrified accusation to give it form.

"The assumption is," he continued, "that your sister is demented, and that conveniently eliminates the need for a motive. I happen to think it's just a little too convenient. Maybe I'm old-fashioned, but whenever I find a murdered corpse, I start digging around for somebody with a logical reason for wanting it that way."

"But if Wilma's insane—"

"Insane is a pretty strong term, Mr. Rathjen. If you had my job, you'd stop thinking of your sister as a freak. This city is crawling with frightened people just like her. Maybe they've lost a loved one and can't get used to being alone;

maybe they've just committed the terrible sin of getting old and unemployable. One way or the other, they're left with a lot of time on their hands and too many scare artists screaming in their ears. A lot of shoddy merchandise is being peddled by fear these days, and it's lonely people like your sister who pay the tax."

All this talk about loneliness seemed to make Curtis uncomfortable. He squirmed like a kid being kept after school. "If Wilma's been lonely, it's her own doing," he protested. "I've done everything I could for her. I offered her a room here in my own house after Mother died, but she can't get along with my wife. Then I fixed up the apartment for her, got her a job so she could be a little more independent, and when she was sick I sent her to the very best doctor—"

"—and spent a lot of money." Osgood sighed. "That's the usual procedure. When the noise outside shatters the conscious mind, turn the victim over to a specialist who can shatter the unconscious as well. To me it makes about as much sense as battering down all the doors of a house and then wondering why the occupant is nervous, but then I'm only a policeman, and I want to know who's been doing such a good job of trying to frame your sister."

A statement like that could make quite a hole in the conversation. Osgood was getting way out on a limb and he knew it; but that was the only way to find out if the limb would hold. Now that Curtis Rathjen was thoroughly confused, he could get down to the purpose of his visit. Osgood was learning more about the art of selling all the time.

"How well did you know Jeri Lynn?" he asked.

Curtis blushed like a Victorian teen-ager. "Why, why, not at all. She was just a tenant. My rentals are all handled through the office."

"Even the nonpaying kind?"

"Now see here, if you're insinuating—"

"I'm not insinuating anything, Mr. Rathjen, but there are a few things I know for a fact. Number one, Jeri Lynn was broke; number two, she didn't leave her job because of ill health—she was fired; number three, the job she was fired from was in a club owned by you—"

"I only own the property," Rathjen protested. "I have nothing to do with the business!"

"—number four, broke as she was, she'd been bragging about a wealthy friend who was putting an end to all her financial troubles."

By this time Curtis wasn't red any more; he was purple. He struggled to his feet, a grotesque, pudgy little man who'd lost every trace of dignity. "So that's what you've come here to do!" he screamed. "To ruin me if you can! Why can't people leave me alone? All my life I've slaved to make something of myself and provide for my family—"

"I'm not trying to ruin anyone except a murderer," Osgood interrupted. "And if your indulgence of Miss Lynn's debt is as innocent as you claim, then at least you can see how it feels to have the evidence pile up against you. Everything I said about you is as true as what is being said about your sister. She did have that cake in her cupboard, and I think I know why. She did leave fingerprints on a glass of whisky in Ruby Lennox's apartment, and I don't know why—not any more than I know why she would know there was a tire iron in the trunk of Ann Jenner's sedan when Ann Jenner didn't know it herself!

"No, Mr. Rathjen, *all* the evidence isn't on one side. Jeri Lynn died on the eve of some event that was to make a great change in her life; I don't think that was a coincidence. She died on the eve of her husband's return from overseas, and I don't think that was a coincidence either. When I asked how well you knew Miss Lynn it was because someone knew her well enough to know about both of these events—and knew your sister well enough to know she'd make a natural suspect if anything went wrong."

Osgood had seen fish with the same expression as Curtis's. They usually had a hook in their mouths. "Then you think my sister is innocent?" he asked weakly.

"I do," Osgood said.

"Well, well, that's wonderful news."

"But I have to prove it. That's why I need your help."

When Osgood put the matter in that light, there wasn't much a devoted brother could do but give straight answers even if the answers concerned the unwelcome subject of Jeri Lynn. Old man Timm had revealed that Curtis was with the girl the night she collapsed, true or false? True, admitted Curtis, but only because he'd come about the rent. Then she was in arrears *before* her collapse? True again, but what did all this have to do with the death of Ruby Lennox? It was a good question, but Osgood insisted on taking one death at a time.

"And when Miss Lynn collapsed that evening you ran across the court to fetch Doctor Fergus, is that right?"

Curtis nodded. "She said there was a doctor visiting at Miss Jenner's apartment."

"A friend of Jeri's?"

"I don't think they'd ever met until he came to attend to her. See here, Sergeant, what are you driving at?"

Osgood didn't answer. He was too busy remembering the way Tony Carmen had run off at the mouth last night. "That little schemer was never sick a day of her life unless it was a hang-over," he'd said. Maybe Tony was right. A clever actress should be able to fake a few symptoms, especially with an eviction hanging in the balance. And a girl who could talk a landlord like Curtis Rathjen out of his rent had to be talented. But there was such a thing as overplaying a part. Jeri must have learned that the hard way.

There was nothing more Curtis could do for Osgood now except to make one telephone call. After that he could go back to his grapefruit juice, if his hand would stop trembling enough to hold the glass.

When Osgood left Curtis Rathjen's house, he drove directly to a chrome-and-plate-glass creation on Wilshire Boulevard and invaded the offices of the Rathjen Realty Company. It was a bloodless invasion because Curtis had called ahead and given the green light. This was the new Curtis Rathjen, subdued, co-operative, and puzzled.

Osgood spent a couple of hours poring over the files. Jeri Lynn had lived in the court for almost a year and a half. Of the tenants now in residence only Ann Jenner and the old man had been there longer. Timm, a helpful secretary explained, was more or less of a fixture. "He comes in handy when there's maintenance work on any of the properties." As for the others, only Tony Carmen had been around as long as a year. The girls from the little theater and the late Ruby Lennox seemed to be the kind who never completely unpacked.

There were others, too. Names of tenants who had come and gone in Jeri's year and a half, and Osgood checked them all: names, occupations, references. It was tedious work, but it had to be done, because it was one thing to catch a man in a lie and quite another thing to prove it. It was even more difficult when so many people lied for so many different reasons.

When his bookwork was done, Osgood went home for lunch and then worked in the yard for a while. Yard work was good for a man with a problem, and Osgood's problems came in litters. The sales talk he'd given Curtis sounded convincing while he was giving it, but it wasn't enough to save a frightened woman with a genius for doing the wrong thing. The minute he showed up at headquarters with the story he had now, Curtis's question would be thrown right in his teeth. What did all this have to do with Ruby Lennox? The sad truth was that without Ruby's death they still had no clear-cut case of murder, and with Ruby's death all of Osgood's theories hit a blank wall.

He had a lot of theories. Rathjen's rental file had contributed quite a bit to Tony's midnight revelations. Timm, Tony, Ann Jenner (and of course the doctor), as well as Curtis Rathjen could have known about Jeri's marriage. They could have seen her with Blade at the court, as the old man had already admitted, or they could have seen the two of them at La Rene's Place. It was interesting how everything came back to La Rene's. Jeri had worked there; Curtis owned the property; Tony wanted to play a trumpet; the doctor's office was just across the parking lot; old man Timm had made a Saturday night visit—Osgood thought about all of those things for a while and then put away his garden tools. Maybe he was raking in the wrong yard.

It was midafternoon when Osgood parked his old sedan behind Tony Carmen's long convertible. It was a kind of hybrid model with a custom-built body and a mechanic's mixture under the hood, but it did dress up the court. The court needed dressing up today. There was a chill in the rising wind that discouraged the usual lawn decoration of live models, and the twin rows of closed windows and doors gave the place an air of having been deserted en masse. But not every door was closed. He'd no more than hit the sidewalk when Osgood became intrigued with the activity outside Jeri Lynn's apartment.

The sidewalk was almost blocked with boxes and suitcases, and as Osgood approached, old man Timm appeared in the doorway with a wastepaper basket in one hand and a mink coat thrown over his arm.

"What the devil's going on here?" Osgood demanded "Who gave you permission to take anything out of that apartment?"

Timm's face wrinkled like a withered apple. "Nobody gave me permission," he said. "I got orders."

"Not from me!"

"Of course not. You don't own this place. Rathjen owns it, and he wants it ready to rent the first of the month. I'm just moving everything to the garage like he told me."

That was just dandy. In the face of this big cleanup the possibility of unearthing any missing evidence in that apartment seemed remote. And now that he thought about it, Osgood remembered that something must be missing.

"You didn't tell me you had a key for this place," he said.

"Sure, I've got a key. I've got a key for all the places so's I can get in to fix things."

"That's right, you're a great little fixer, aren't you, Pop? I should have thought of that before."

By this time Osgood was poking through that wastebasket in the old man's hand. The unpaid bills were there, and the blotters, and a couple of old newspapers.

"What's this all about?" Timm demanded. "What are you looking for?"

"Letters," Osgood said, because now he knew what it was that was missing. He'd really known all this time— right from the first day. Bills but no letters, photographs but no snapshots, and yet here was a girl with a husband overseas. "One letter in particular," he added, "one from her soldier husband."

"She never kept letters," the old man declared. "Threw 'em all out in the trash. I burned her letters all the time."

"Before or after reading?"

It was sad how careless people could get when the pressure was off. Because Wilma Rathjen had run away from Ruby's body, Phillip Blade could walk into headquarters and sing his heart out about that generous letter he'd written his wife. And now, because Wilma Rathjen was behind bars, old man Timm could admit that he burned

Jeri's mail. The guilt was spread over his face like blackerry jam.

"This particular letter no wife would throw out in the trash," Osgood added, "because it would make such good evidence—"

He didn't have a chance to finish. "That's crazy!" the old man yelled. "A soldier overseas can put anything into letter. That don't make him a murderer!"

Careless was no word for it. Osgood looked at the old man and grinned. "—good evidence for a divorce trial," he concluded, "unless there was something a lot different in that letter than what Blade says he wrote."

The old man looked awfully silly standing there with the wastebasket and the mink coat and the jam on his face. He didn't seem to have a word to say, but then it wasn't his turn to speak because the voices on the walk had aroused the interest of a khaki-clad figure who now appeared in Jeri's doorway.

"Why don't you ask him?" Blade said.

Osgood looked up at a very angry face. He was a little surprised to see Blade here, although he had more right than the old man.

"Why don't you leave the old man alone?" the kid added. "He's had enough trouble because of me."

"Meaning the fracas outside La Rene's Saturday night?"

Blade's face reddened. "How did you know about that?"

"I didn't know until you told me. Where did she keep the letter, Timm? It wasn't in the desk because I looked there myself. Come to think of it, I believe that's where Blade was looking the day we walked in on him."

"I don't know what you're talking about," the old man said.

"No? And I don't suppose you'd know what I was talking about if I told you that Wilma Rathjen saw a couple of prowlers down here the night after Jeri's body was found."

"That crazy woman could see anything!"

"She even saw the face of one of them."

Osgood was stretching things a bit, but sometimes a man had to stretch to make a story go around. Phillip Blade had a cigarette in his mouth. He took it out and tossed it to the sidewalk. "Come on, let's get this stuff out of here," he said to Timm. "I've got to get back to the base—if the sergeant can spare me." He walked back inside the apartment, and the old man walked out to the garage, but Osgood didn't do a thing to stop them. He just stood there and watched that cigarette burn down to a long ash, and then he turned around and headed upstairs to Wilma's apartment.

A man had to be pretty desperate, Osgood told himself, to go looking for any clue as flimsy as Wilma's carefully hoarded cigarette butt. Even if he did prove that Blade had been the prowler outside the window, he was just going to stumble over Ruby's bloody body again, and that was getting a little exasperating. For of all possible suspects, Phillip Blade had the least reason for killing Ruby. He'd never even seen her.

At the top of the stairs Osgood went to work with his skeleton key. He felt a little nervous about it, as if Wilma's eyes might be watching and her piercing scream might ring out at any moment, just as it had the night a camera artist wandered up on her roof. But only a yellow cat met Osgood, ecstatic at the possibility of being fed. Alice knew what humans were for. When the door was opened, she went straight to the refrigerator, but Osgood went straight to the desk. Top drawer, right-hand side. He knew exactly where to look because he'd been peering over Wilma's shoulder when she brought out her treasure Saturday night. It was still there, but by the time he found it Osgood was no longer interested.

Something new had been added to the contents of that drawer. Something stranger than a cigarette butt and more damaging than a long-lost cake. Osgood stared at his discovery with ice in his stomach—two ragged pieces of a torn photo that fitted together like the knot of a noose, because there was no doubt about the identity of the model. The hair was bleached, and she hadn't smiled that way on a slab at the morgue; but it was Jeri Lynn. Jeri Lynn in a pose that belonged on a barracks wall or a firehouse calendar—but never ripped in two and hidden away in Wilma Rathjen's desk!

Osgood dropped down on the little maple chair and tried to understand. Any picture of the dead girl in Wilma's desk would have been suspicious, but this one had been torn in anger. It was going to make Frenchy's sin-killer theory sound like gospel. And maybe Frenchy was right. "What is this between you and the old girl?" he mocked again, and now that nobody was reading his mind Osgood could search for an answer. Call it pity, call it self-recognition—something about the woman must have struck home. There were people on earth so tied to duty that even when the ropes were removed the scars remained—that's what John Peter Osgood knew about Wilma Rathjen, and more. He knew the pleasure of smashing a fist into Tony Carmen, rope-free Tony Carmen, and it came to him with a kind of horror that the satisfaction of that blow was a blood brother to this torn photo. The young, the arrogant, the beautiful— Osgood had fists and a badge in his pocket, but Wilma Rathjen had a window. Maybe that's what Frenchy had known all along, and what John Peter Osgood didn't want to know.

But Jeri Lynn hadn't been smashed. That simple truth moved in to challenge Osgood's doubt. Jeri had died clean and carefully in a manufactured sleep; only her picture had been destroyed in anger. And what was it about that picture that had been so obvious the instant he opened the drawer? Saturday night, that was the thing. Saturday night there had been no picture, only a cigarette stub and a frightened woman telling a story she was forced to tell because she'd been caught coming through Ann Jenner's hedges.

Osgood thought about that for a long time. Then he thought about a birthday cake, a couple of prowlers, and all the lies and evasions that could put a man off the track even though he knew from the beginning that Jeri Lynn had too many friends and not enough mourners. And now it seemed that one of her friends was an art collector. For the first time he had a tangible link between Jeri and a possible killer, and he was going to trace that link to its source if it took all night.

He pocketed the torn photo and started toward the door. It was almost night now, and the early dusk that had crept over the room as he sat at Wilma's desk was filled with howls when he tried to leave. Alice had lungs like a prima donna.

"All right, shut up," Osgood muttered. "I'll get you some milk."

The refrigerator was just behind the shutter-screen partition, but when he opened the door the interior was like a pocket. The bulb must have burned out. He reached for the wall switch. A copper-plated lamp dangled from the ceiling and a pair of matching brackets flanked the sink, but nothing happened. He flipped the switch a couple of times and then pursued the matter further: living room, bedroom, bath. There were no lights anywhere in the apartment. No lights—and Wilma Rathjen, who was afraid to enter a dark apartment alone, had fled in the middle of the night.

It was amazing what could be seen in the dark. Osgood came down the steps at a dead run. In front of the garage he almost collided with the old man and Tony Carmen, who seemed to be insisting that a garage was a place for parking cars. "Where's the fuse box?" Osgood yelled, but even without an answer he knew where to look. Ruby

Lennox had occupied the first apartment at the foot of Wilma's stairs, and Ruby had died at the south end of the garage.

It was a relay switch arrangement with the lever to one of the lines still flipped to the off position. That was just one more mistake by a killer who had made too many. One touch of a thumb and Osgood was grinning up at Wilma's bright windows like a kid before a Christmas tree. With all that light he'd never stumble over Ruby's body again.

Now he could get to work on that photograph.

CHAPTER EIGHTEEN

Wilma sat very still on the edge of a straight-backed chair and smiled at her shoes. It was so nice to have her own back again; it would have been even nicer if she could have had her own coat instead of the dark-blue one the matron loaned her; but that was because of the trip from the hospital to this stuffy room where so many excited people made such a lot of noise. Wilma only vaguely understood what was happening. She was out of it, somehow, a mere bystander at the conflict of what was to be done with her.

It was all a waste of time anyway. At first she'd tried to explain and answer the questions that came like steady rain. Did she remember the cake? Jeri Lynn's birthday cake? Of course she remembered. She'd taken the order, hadn't she? "I don't know why, but I can't get it out of my mind that I did something wrong with it," she said. Then all the important people, the doctors and the lawyers and the policemen (and Curtis, who was surely the most important of all), began to look at one another and gravely nod their heads.... And what about Ruby Lennox? Did she remember Ruby? Wilma's eyes grew moist. "It was the lights," she said. "The lights went out." Then everybody looked grave and nodded again. It was all a complete waste of time.

But they were very nice to her. It was wonderful how nice people could be when they thought you were crazy. When she asked for her shoes, they were brought to her. Some thoughtful person had found them at the theater and turned them in, and she asked Curtis to give the man a quarter. A little later she requested a glass of water, and one of the policemen fetched it right away. She didn't ask Curtis to give him anything because that would be bribery; but it all went to prove how she could have anything she asked for now that she had decided to be crazy—anything but freedom.

Wilma thought about these things while she smiled at her shoes, because they were the only things worth thinking about. To argue was useless; to explain was hopeless. When they first brought her into the room, dazed and drowsy still from the effects of heavy sedation, she had looked about for Sergeant Osgood the way any stranger in a crowd looks for a familiar face. But Sergeant Osgood wasn't there, and that meant that she had no friends at all. It was then that Wilma decided to die—in her own way.

The conversation in the room was a steady din, but now and then a door would open into one of the corridors and a great sweep of noisy confusion washed in like an angry wave against the walls. Wilma knew all about the corridor. She had caught a glimpse of that turmoil when the matron brought her up in the elevator; it was filled with reporters, cameramen, and curiosity seekers; it was all the officer at the door could do to hold them back. Sooner or later they would get the official word that Curtis Rathjen's sister was an insane killer and what a holiday they would have then! What a confusion in that corridor!

Wilma's smile went underground. She sat quietly for a

few minutes longer, thinking things no one must read on her face, but no one except the matron even noticed her any more. She didn't look much like a matron, but then Wilma had never seen a matron before except in newspaper pictures, and even then she always had to read the caption to know which woman was the criminal. She added that to her collection of thoughts, carefully buttoned the matron's coat, and then began to slump down on her chair.

The matron was at her side in an instant.

"I hate to bother you," Wilma said weakly, "but I think I'm going to be sick."

It was a crisis, of course. Not a major crisis because Curtis's lawyer was in heated debate with the police psychiatrist and none of the important people could be disturbed; but the matron spoke to one policeman, and he spoke to another. Seconds later both Wilma and the matron were eased into the corridor through the side door. Just around the corner were the elevators and the reporters.

"The washroom is this way," the matron said, but Wilma was already making a right-hand turn.

"Miss Rathjen—come back!"

That was the way with people who still argued with the inevitable; they became excited and cried out when something went wrong. What went wrong for the matron was that her weak and ailing charge suddenly wasn't weak and ailing any more; she was strong enough to break away and march right toward that crowd of reporters. The moment she was in full view of them she whirled about and took up the matron's cry.

"Don't you pull away from me, Wilma Rathjen! Come back here!"

It was the call for a general stampede, and Wilma barely managed to dart back against the elevators away from the crowd. By the time the down elevator opened its door, an army of noisy, milling people separated her from the bewildered matron and the flash bulbs were going off like fireworks.

"What's going on up there?" the elevator man asked on the trip down.

"It's that Rathjen woman," Wilma said. "She tried to escape."

"You don't say! She *must* be crazy!"

"Yes," Wilma answered, "there's no doubt about it. Main floor, please."

She walked through the lobby and out to the street. A row of taxicabs was lined up at the curb, and she got into the first one. The driver dropped his newspaper on the seat beside him and had the motor running before he asked the question: "Where to, lady?"

Wilma gave him her address in a calm, clear voice. Once they were under way she leaned back in the seat and closed her eyes. She didn't want to open them again until she could look out at her own familiar neighborhood.

The neighborhood was very familiar to Osgood. It was just about the same time yesterday that he'd barged into Fergus's office and what turned out to be a very enlightening conversation, but not quite enlightening enough. This trip he found the nurse at her own desk where she belonged, but it didn't look as if she intended to remain there long.

"I really can't talk to you now," she insisted. "The doctor has an out patient, and I promised to pick up Donnie at the nursery school. I'm late now."

"So am I," Osgood said, "About twenty-four hours late. Didn't you leave something out of that story you told me yesterday?"

There was an old Chinese proverb about the worth of one picture, and it seemed to hold true where Ann Jenner was concerned. When the two-piece photograph met her eyes, she stared at it as if it had fallen from outer space.

"Where did you get that?" she gasped.

"It came from your apartment, didn't it?"

"Yes, but it wasn't torn. It was in my desk."

"Why?"

"I don't know really—yes, I do know. Jeri gave it to me the night I brought the sleeping pills. She had it in her hand when she came out of the bedroom. She said an old admirer had given it to her and laughed about it."

Ann's voice had dropped to a whisper. "I don't know why I kept it," she added.

"Maybe so you could show it to Doctor Fergus," Osgood suggested.

"Why should I do that?"

"Well, offhand I'd say in hopes of convincing him that she wasn't the proper wife for a promising young doctor. What would you say, Miss Jenner?"

"No, that's not true! Arnold never intended to marry that girl. She only thought—"

It was the nurse's own hand across her mouth that stopped the angry flow of words. Mouths could be so troublesome, particularly when they weren't full-lipped, provocative mouths like Jeri Lynn's had been. But eyes could speak, too.

"She only thought what?" Osgood asked.

He wasn't going to get an answer, of course. It would take time to thaw out that frozen silence, and time was the one thing Osgood couldn't spare. But it was a little silly for the nurse to stand there like a model for "speak no evil." She'd already told him what he wanted to know.

He left the medical building and crossed the parking lot to the phone booth outside the market. Between Tony's outburst last night and Ann Jenner's amended story today, he'd covered a lot of territory. The picture was beginning to be as clear as those larger-than-life portraits on La Rene's billboards across the lot, because all it had really needed was the proper lighting. Wilma—not Ruby Lennox. That was the story that made all the difference. He had time to think about that while waiting for his call to go through, because there seemed to be a lot of confusion at headquarters. Then Frenchy came on.

"Where have you been all day?" he bawled. "You've missed all the excitement."

"Maybe I'll have some soon," Osgood muttered, "as soon as you get an address for me."

What Osgood wanted was a simple matter: the address on the card of a commercial photographer that was still tucked inside Jeri's phone book. In due time he got it, along with the latest news bulletin. "Your girl friend just walked out," Frenchy reported. "Right in the middle of her psycho examination. The hunt is on again."

Osgood didn't pause in his note-taking. "Good for her," he said, and hung up.

The address turned out to be a couple of rooms over a used-furniture store on Western Avenue. There was a flight of half-lighted stairs and then a frosted-glass door with some lettering in chipped paint: *Fine-Art Foto Service, Hunter Poole, Pres.* At this hour Osgood feared the door might be locked, but the knob turned in his hand, and a light from the back room spilled out over a marked lack of prosperity. Hunter Poole, from the looks of that front office, was very likely office boy, mailing clerk, and janitor as well as president of the firm. The long counter that ran along one side of the room was cluttered with dusty back issues of photography magazines, and the score of glossy prints tacked at random on the plywood walls were in a category not far removed from the item in Osgood's coat pocket. Even in so dim a light the comparison was favorable, and the more he studied the prints the more excited he became.

But Osgood's study period was cut short when a little man in shirt sleeves poked his head through the studio doorway just long enough to recognize this ardent student of his art. It was a case of look and run, with Osgood making a fast leap over the counter in sudden pursuit. Hunter Poole looked no more like a prexy than his office looked like a legitimate business firm; but he did resemble exactly the man who searched for camera angles on Wilma Rathjen's roof.

Wilma looked up at the roof as she stepped out of the cab. The sun had gone down, but the afterglow still painted a yellow sky behind the ridgepole, and against the sky she could see the silhouette of a golden-edged cat. Alice was waiting for her to come home. Faithful—and hungry—Alice. The thought of having been missed, by anything at all, filled Wilma's heart with a terrible happiness that faded when the cab driver spoke.

"Say, ain't this the street where that crazy woman lives? The one in all the newspapers?"

"I don't read the newspapers any more," Wilma said.

"I think you've got something there, lady... That'll be three-sixty."

Wilma didn't have so much as a penny on her, but at that instant Ann Jenner's door swung open, and the nurse peered out at the new arrival. "Is that you, Arnold?" she called, and then fell silent at the sight of Wilma and the cab driver.

"Oh, Miss Jenner," Wilma cried, "just a moment, please."

The nurse wasn't going anywhere. She seemed to have grown to the doorknob.

"I wonder if you have a few dollars handy for the cab driver? It'll save me running up and down stairs and the meter keeps running, you know."

"A few dollars?" Ann repeated, weakly.

"Yes. Three-sixty, isn't it, driver? Please give him an extra quarter for the tip. He drove very nicely."

Wilma left the transaction in Ann's hands and trotted on down the center walk. She was vaguely aware of other doors opening along the way, and of other faces peering out at her as she passed. It had been bold to impose on the nurse that way, but she didn't want to run the gantlet of that long walk more than once. Ann would get her money back. She would make a note of it for Curtis.

"Miss Rathjen, wait a minute—"

It was annoying to have the woman scream out her presence to the entire courtyard. Wilma had hoped to arrive by cover of dusk, but now she had to wait at the foot of the stairs while Ann caught up with her.

"I'll see that you get your money back in the morning," she said crossly, but Ann just looked annoyed.

"Hang the money! What about you, Miss Rathjen? Are you all right?"

"Of course I'm all right! Now if you'll please pay the driver—"

"I paid the driver! He's paid and gone! But what about the police? Did they let you go?"

Wilma steadied herself against the railing and drew up tall. This was one of the hazards she'd anticipated. With such a short distance remaining, no one was going to stop her now.

"Oh, that's all been straightened out," she said brightly. "My brother has taken care of everything."

Ann Jenner's voice called her a liar, but her tongue wasn't quite sure. "I don't see how—" she began.

"Why not? My brother is a very important man, Miss Jenner. Even you have admitted that. Now, if you'll excuse me, I must get upstairs and feed poor Alice."

Wilma left Ann Jenner staring openmouthed at the foot of the stairs. There was such a little way left to go....

CHAPTER NINETEEN

"Well, what do you make of that?" Ann exclaimed.

She wasn't talking to herself. By this time six troubled people were gathered together in the courtyard; six troubled faces all turned upward toward the roof.

"Do you suppose she was telling the truth?" Blade wondered aloud.

"If she was it's the first time," the old man muttered.

"I'm not so sure," Tony said. "You know how it is with these big shots. They can do anything and get away with it. Just let us be in that old girl's shoes and we'd never see daylight again!"

One by one the lights appeared at the upstairs windows, and their very appearance seemed to give weight to Tony's words. There was a kind of finality about them. It was inconceivable that anyone still a fugitive could return so casually and make herself at home in so normal a manner. Of course Tony was right; Curtis Rathjen was a man of influence.

"I don't know," Ann murmured, "I think we should call the police and make sure."

"The police!" Timm snorted. "I've seen how the police handle things—fool questions—nosing around—trying to make trouble for innocent folks. Bring the police out here again and Rathjen will blow his top!"

"But we have to do something!"

"All right then, I'll call Rathjen and see what he says. I've got his home number in case anything should go wrong. If this ain't something gone wrong I hope I never see it!"

The old man scurried back into his apartment, and Sharl breathed a vehement: "You can say that again! We may all be murdered in our beds before morning!"

"In our beds?" cried Denise. "Who's going to bed with a crazy woman over our heads? She doesn't like me. I just know she doesn't like me!"

It was a sobering thought, The courtyard convention discussed the situation a bit longer and then agreed to adjourn until the old man reported on his call. It was getting too chilly to wait outside. The wind was rising like an advance agent for another winter storm, and a crumpled newspaper from a box of trash outside the garage spiraled ghostlike against the darkening sky. Ann shuddered.

"I'm going in and call Doctor Fergus, too," she said. "Maybe he'll know what to do."

But Tony already had everything figured out. "Just keep your doors and windows locked and don't go outside no matter what you hear," he said. "That's what Jeri and Ruby didn't do."

Wilma was no more aware of the furor in the courtyard than she was of a scene being enacted in a brightly lighted room just a few miles away.

Hunter Poole squirmed on his chair like a small boy trying to get the teacher's attention. But Poole didn't want to recite. He wanted to leave the room, the building, even the city if such a thing had been possible, because it was some pretty choice camera work the raiding party was bringing in from that studio over the used-furniture store. He could have made a small fortune peddling it to a market that knew no depressions; but now it was just going to give eyestrain to some judge before he passed sentence, and this seemed eminently unfair to Hunter Poole.

"Well, what's it going to be?" Osgood demanded. "A fine and a few months or a reserved seat in the gas chamber?"

"Gas chamber!" Poole scoffed. "Nobody gets the pill for peddling pictures!"

"No, but they get the pill for murder."

"So who's committed murder?"

"That's what I'm trying to find out. It could be you."

Poole tried to laugh, but it was just a hollow rattle in his throat. He wanted a cigarette but knew better than to ask for it. At least that little cop the big one called "Frenchy" might stop blowing smoke in his face.

"I'll go over everything just once more," Osgood said. "Here we have a torn photograph of one Jeri Lynn, deceased. You've already admitted having taken that photo a couple of years ago."

"That's right," Poole agreed. "What of it? It's a good shot."

"That's all in how you want to look at it. It isn't such a good shot for a girl trying to convince a respectable boy friend that she'd make a good wife and mother."

"Is that my grief? I paid her to pose. She had no gun in her back."

"But she's dead now."

"A lot of people are dead now. What's that to me?"

Hunter Poole's argument might have sounded more convincing if he hadn't had such a sickly pallor. The pallor made the bruise on his jaw a kind of dirty purples and it wasn't a fresh bruise because Osgood hadn't used that kind of force on him. He was afraid the little guy might break.

"It might be a lot to you," Osgood insisted. "Would you like to hear how it's going to sound to a jury? We've got a D.A. who can make it sound awfully good. First he'll tell about Jeri Lynn, a poor kid down on her luck who's forced to pose for trashy pin-ups to earn a living—"

"You're breaking my heart!" Poole snorted.

"—but finally she gets a break, of sorts, and lands a dancing job at La Rene's Place—until her health fails."

"That little tramp was healthy as a horse!"

Osgood almost smiled. For a man who professed no knowledge of Jeri Lynn, Poole was being very outspoken.

"Then at last she met a respectable and well-to-do suitor who could take her out of all that squalor for good; but Hunter Poole has a stack of negatives she might not want her respectable suitor to know about, and he sees a chance to pick up a few dollars via the blackmail route."

"Blackmail!" Poole screamed. "So that's it! So the old goat told you!"

The break had come. Everyone in the room sensed it: Osgood, Frenchy, the lieutenant, anyone who wasn't out chasing Wilma again. Curtis Rathjen had taken his high-salaried retinue and departed shortly after Wilma's un-scheduled exit, and so he missed hearing Poole's descriptive adjectives as he blurted out the story of an attempt to turn an unflattering likeness into ready cash.

"But it was only for laughs," he said. "I never col-lected."

"Is that how you bruised your jaw, laughing?"

Osgood's question brought Poole's left hand up to his jaw. "Look," he sputtered, "I told you once, I told you a dozen times, I don't know anything about Jeri Lynn's death! The day after her body was found I got a telephone call—anonymous. 'There's an interesting view from the roof of the garage at that court where the Lynn girl died,' the voice said. 'Maybe you could sell it to the papers.' Well, business was slow so I went out to have a look. I couldn't even get near the roof with that old girl watching all the time, so I had to wait until it began to get dark."

"And until I went into the bathroom of that apartment and turned on the light," Osgood added.

"That was an accident. That just happened. But right away I got the idea of what that voice on the phone meant and took the picture I gave you the next day. Then the old girl started screaming, and you know the rest."

Poole was exhausted. He slumped back in his chair and Osgood watched him sweat. When a man was that scared, it was hard to tell the truth from a lie; but out of that frantic story one truth was plain—whatever else that shot from the roof was meant to accomplish, it must have terrified a killer who forgot to draw the shade.

And maybe Poole was right. Maybe Osgood did know the rest.

"Who made that phone call, Poole?" he demanded.

The little man moistened his lips. "I told you once, I told you a dozen times—"

"You haven't told me a thing, but now I'm going to tell you! You know who called you, and by this time you've figured out why. It was because a killer was nervous. A killer who couldn't remember that the woman on the roof worked late Tuesday night, and who had to know what she might have seen because the police were asking questions. But the picture you took of that window only made the fear worse, until finally it seemed necessary to seal her lips with a tire iron."

Osgood wasn't talking only to Poole. This was for the lieutenant, for Frenchy, and for all the smart people in the world who knew all the answers. He wanted no interruptions. There had been a little something going on at the door, but he shrugged off the tug at his arm.

"This is your anonymous caller, Poole, a frightened killer who could feel safe only if Wilma Rathjen was dead."

And then Frenchy spoiled the whole build-up.

"There's a cabby outside who says he just drove the old girl home," he said. "I wonder how the killer likes that."

There was so little time. That was the only thing that bothered Wilma now. She would have liked to sit down in the big wing chair and relax while Alice sang a welcome-home song in her lap. She would have liked to turn on the radio—not to the raucous voices that made the world so frightening, but to something soft and soothing to think by. There were so many things she didn't understand, and perhaps if she could just sit quietly and think them all out they would fall into place. But this was the way of life. The dreary days followed one another like convicts in a chain gang, and then suddenly it was the end of the chain and there was so little time.

She had no illusions about her escape. It was only because such a thing was hopeless that she'd managed it at all, and any moment now the sirens would scream and the police would come swarming up the stairs. She must be ready for them.

Wilma smiled wistfully at the soft light patterns the lamps made on her lovely things. It didn't seem strange that the lights were working again—that's how they were supposed to be. It was annoying to find the refrigerator door standing open, but at least poor Alice had been able to forage for herself. One cupboard door stood ajar, and when she looked inside, she could see that the cake was gone, but that was no cause for grief. She'd never wanted it there anyway. She did frown as she closed the drawer that had been left open on her desk, but the fact that her apartment had been invaded was no longer important. The important thing was to put everything in order while there was still time, and that included going to her closet and removing all those paper bags from her clothing because they were a matter between herself and an old fear— not a detail to excite the curiosity of strangers.

While she attended to these chores, Wilma considered her problem. Gas was the easiest and the neatest, but it might be too slow. There was a length of clothesline in the broom closet, if one knew how to tie knots, and an array of knives in the kitchen that would probably stain the linoleum: but she rejected these, too. What was needed was something fast and certain—surely her crowded medicine chest would hold the answer.

She had no fear. It was as if fear and anger were the same; when one was spent, the other was bankrupt, and she'd squandered her anger on the broken image of an evil face.... All of that came back to her when she went into the bathroom and reached toward the chest. Her hands were bruised and scarred—that was the first thing. Transfixed, she stared at the image of her own face in the medicine chest mirror. This chin, this mouth, these eyes— they were all her own familiar features. No line and no expression but what belonged to her. And yet last night Wilma Rathjen had been the evil twin of an orange-haired harlot!

The gods men worship have written their names upon their faces.

It was an old forgotten wisdom that mocked Wilma from the mirror. She tried to back away and could not. If the face of a thief had been her own, what had she stolen to put such evil there? She had lied about the schoolteacher, but surely she'd been punished for that. She'd stolen those things from the theater—and left her own in return. She'd taken Jeri Lynn's cake and not told Sergeant Osgood even when he asked, but only because she was so afraid of what Curtis might do.

Curtis. The mirror gave back the name of her wickedness even if her mind rebelled. That evil face returned again, and this time she knew that it could not be destroyed with blows. This time she studied it carefully and tried to remember a time when she hadn't hated her brother....

There were no hands on the clock. Wilma never knew how long she stood there staring at the thief in her mirror. She never knew which sound it was that aroused her— the shouting in the courtyard below that seemed, once she became aware of it, to have been going on for some time, or the howls of a yellow cat clawing at the outside door. But she knew the shouting must mean the police.

It seemed a shame to have to go now when she was just beginning to make a great discovery. She wanted to study that face in the mirror longer; but from the moment of her capture she'd planned this way out. The important thing, the only thing was to make sure that she'd never be locked up again. She opened the door of the cabinet and went hurriedly through the many bottles, but the shouts grew louder, and the cat howled more pitifully. Since she'd never be able to do another thing for Alice, she could at least let her out—and then one of the kitchen knives would have to suffice.

But when Wilma opened the door for Alice, she was immediately intrigued by the lights. A strange glow filled the sky where the night should be, and the shouts began to filter through that vast distance between what happened to Wilma Rathjen and what happened to the world. She couldn't make out the words, but there was a great deal of excitement that centered on the dancing light. Then the rude finger of reality gouged her into awareness. The light was from a fire, and the fire was directly beneath her in that catchall garage!

For some minutes Wilma had anticipated the fires of hell, but she didn't expect them so quickly. There was only one stair and that—when she approached it—was a tunnel of flames. The cat could leap from the roof deck to the roof of the next-door garage, but Wilma was trapped.

"Look, there she is!" cried a voice from below. "She's built herself a funeral pyre!"

The cry was as fantastic as the fire itself, and suddenly Wilma knew that she didn't want to die. Not like this. Not like a sacrificial animal burned alive for the appeasement of the mob! She ran to the railing and looked down. Below her was a swarm of excited little people with horrified faces that appeared and disappeared in billows of smoke. She didn't care if they were policemen; she wanted down!

"Miss Rathjen, Miss Rathjen, over here!"

Whirling about, Wilma caught sight of something moving against the railing at the rear of the building—a ladder. Someone had placed a ladder against the closed side of the garage where the flames hadn't reached. She didn't have to be called a second time. She was across the roof and over the railing almost before the ladder was in place.

It was too late then for caution.

CHAPTER TWENTY

When the ladder swung out into space, Wilma grasped the railing and held on with both hands. It was a terrible tug of war that she couldn't hope to win because someone with much greater strength was pulling against her. Finger by finger her grip lessened until the ladder was perpendicular and she had no defense left but a scream. She was still screaming when the shouts and the running footsteps came below.

"Never mind the man!" someone shouted. "Grab that ladder!"

The ladder swayed crazily in the air and then settled back against the rail. After that, Wilma wasn't quite sure of anything for some time, and the last thing she remembered was the added weight on the ladder and the strong arms that caught her as she collapsed.

"It's all right now," Osgood said. "It's all over."

Osgood was a little premature. It was quite a while before it was all over, because a gasoline-soaked garage stacked with inflammable articles could give the fire department a lot of trouble in a strong wind. But arson wasn't as simple as a hair dryer dropped in a bathtub, or as quick as a light switch pulled in the night. Too many things could go wrong. The wind could change; the stucco walls could be wet from the recent rains; and a cab driver who read his newspaper could become suspicious of a fare.

And yet it could have worked. That was the thought

that hardened Osgood's mouth as he carried Wilma down the ladder and down the long walk to Ann Jenner's living-room. It could have worked even if the fire hadn't destroyed all trace of the act; for who would have been blamed for such a sloppy crime? Who but a crazy woman lying behind the garage with a broken neck?

Osgood and the nurse were still trying to revive Wilma when Tony Carmen burst into the room. In all that confusion he was just one more shouting voice.

"He got away!" he cried. "I chased him two or three blocks down the alley but he got away!"

"It doesn't matter," Osgood said. "I know who he was."

Inside Ann Jenner's living-room the noise turned off like a button pressed. All that remained was the sound of the firemen working at the back of the lot. That's how it was when Wilma opened her eyes—a kind of unreal quietness and all the white faces frozen in silence around the divan: Ann, Tony, old man Timm, the theatrical girls, even Curtis with a black smudge on one pink cheek and his breath coming hard and quick.

"Are you sure? Did you recognize him?" Curtis asked.

"I didn't have to," Osgood said. "Oh, there you are, Doctor, Come in."

The front door was still open from Tony's sudden entrance, and through it stepped Dr. Fergus, tieless and disheveled. "My God, what's going on here?" he demanded. "Ann, are you all right?"

Because she was so close to the nurse, Wilma saw the way her tense face brightened at the sound of the doctor's words. It was a small thing to notice, but when horror has blocked out all the big things, only the small ones remain.

"It's Miss Rathjen," the nurse said. "Someone tried to kill her. Oh, Arnold!"

It was strange how things worked out. The calm and efficient Ann Jenner had called a doctor for poor Miss Rathjen—and it was she herself who collapsed sobbing on the end of the divan. And it was Dr. Fergus who put his aim about her shoulders, stiffly at first, as if not quite certain what treatment was proper in such a case, and then with a little more warmth.

"Let her cry," Osgood said. "It's about time somebody around here broke down."

"If you've been hounding her again—" Fergus threatened.

"I haven't been hounding anyone; I've only been trying to save an innocent woman's life, and her reason! Confession is supposed to be good for the soul, Miss Jenner. You've tried a couple of doses. Maybe you'd feel better if you went the full distance."

"I told you the truth," Ann gasped between sobs.

"In parts and pieces. You told me about doping that drink of Jeri's and then this afternoon you admitted taking her photograph. But what you so carefully omitted is the nature of your conversation. You weren't really worried about Jeri's health, were you? So far as you were concerned it was entirely too good. And yet you made a special trip back to her apartment to deliver a couple of sleeping pills. Let's see, now; Jeri was in the bedroom presumably speaking on the telephone. 'I can't talk any longer,' she said. 'I've got to meet someone for dinner.' Then apparently she heard you come in and came out of the bedroom with that photograph in her hands. Suppose you take it from there."

Ann wasn't crying any more. She looked at Dr. Fergus, and he nodded. It was like a starting signal.

"I wasn't very complimentary," she admitted, "I asked her if she'd shown it to Arnold. She said—"

"Yes, Miss Jenner?"

"She said it wouldn't make any difference if she did. She said he was so crazy about her nothing anyone could do or say would break them up and that only a fool would try. She said they were going to be married as soon as a few details were arranged—that he was going to propose that night.

"I knew then that the sleeping pills wouldn't straighten anything out, but the drink was already doped. After she fell asleep, I took the photo and went back to my apartment. I called Arnold to tell him Jeri had taken a sedative and couldn't keep their date; then I asked if I could see him. He came over and we went for a drive, but I didn't take the photograph."

"She didn't have to," Fergus broke in. "I told her that night I was tired of Jeri's tricks. She was no more in love with me than she was suffering from a breakdown. I may have been fooled for a while, but I certainly had no intention of proposing to the girl that night or any other! I was just trying to find a way to get rid of her!"

Only the silent listeners could get the full impact of Fergus's words, and Osgood, who was watching the nurse's face all this time, saw where they struck home the hardest. "Is that what you told Miss Jenner?" he asked.

"Well, yes. Something like that."

"And two days later the girl she'd left in a drugged sleep was found dead."

No one could fail to grasp the significance of Osgood's words, but he didn't like to have the floor snatched from under his feet.

"Then it was Fergus—" Tony cried.

"—who was Jeri's prize catch," Osgood interrupted. "The very promising young Doctor Fergus, not Curtis Rathjen at all. And that's important to remember because it tells us something about Jeri Lynn. She was a realist, but she was human. She liked her men attractive as well as well heeled."

It was difficult to tell which implication upset Curtis more, than he was unattractive or that he'd been suspected of an illicit relation with the dead girl. "I wish you'd stop linking my name with that girl!" he protested. "Who would seriously suspect me of such a thing?"

Osgood's stony face turned toward the protestor. "Your sister, for one," he said.

"Wilma!"

"Yes, and I suspect that the sight of the doctor's car pulling away from the curb just as she was arriving home that night had a lot to do with it. The models are similar, you know."

At the moment Curtis shouted her name, Wilma tried to sit up again. This time no one stopped her. In fact, Osgood stepped over and placed a cushion behind her back. "Are you feeling all right now?" he asked. It was the first time there had been any warmth in his voice.

"I think so," Wilma murmured, "but I don't quite understand—"

"You'll understand in a few minutes. I'm going to explain this thing right down from the beginning, just so there won't be any squawks when I make an arrest."

That last word brought back the quiet again. Even Curtis had nothing more to say.

"The beginning," Osgood continued, "was the day we received a call that a dead girl had been found in her bathtub. There was a hair dryer involved, and it began to bother me as soon as it developed that this same girl had spent the last afternoon of her life in a beauty shop with hair dryers and all. Unless she was awfully clumsy, it looked as if that appliance in her bath water had received an assist—and from someone who didn't know where she'd spent her afternoon. To me, that ruled out any woman who wasn't blind in both eyes. A woman would notice a thing like that even if a man wouldn't. It particularly ruled out Ann Jenner because she'd actually driven the girl home from the shop. But of course I didn't know that then.

"So I started looking for a man. To begin with, I was

just looking for a man who didn't worry when his date didn't show; then we added a little beauty-shop gossip about a wealthy suitor Jeri was about to catch one way or another. There was a Cadillac involved, and for a time, I made the same mistake as Miss Rathjen, and I didn't even know that Jeri had been living rent-free."

"I explained that!" Curtis objected. "I explained it two or three times!"

Osgood almost smiled. Jeri Lynn's natural resources could explain it better, but this was no time to start an argument. "That's unimportant for the moment," he said, "because what I'm driving at is the way things stood the day I came out here looking for a missing birthday cake and found Phillip Blade looking for his wife. Blade was a big surprise to me, but not to everybody in this court."

There was a sound of shuffling and coughing that came from the old man in overalls who was edging toward the door. He'd been awfully quiet all this time. Almost as quiet as Blade himself.

"What's your hurry, Pop?" Osgood asked. "You don't have to worry about that letter any more. You burned it, didn't you?"

Wallace Timm's mouth worked nervously. "I burned all her letters," he muttered.

"Including one that wasn't thrown out in the trash. How did you know about it, Timm? How did you know where to look?"

The old man was scared. All that talk about making an arrest was bound to make a man with a secret scared, and when a secret got too hot to hold there was only one thing to do with it.

"I meant no harm," the old man whispered. "I only wanted to put the soldier's mind at rest. I remembered the letter when you asked so many questions the day you found the body. I'd seen it when I fixed the bathroom lock a week or so before. It was a crazy letter, full of threats of what he'd do if she left him. Didn't mean any-thing, but there's no telling what police will think, so that night I took my passkey and went back to her apartment to look for it. Found it under a hatbox in the closet."

"The prowler inside the apartment," Osgood remarked.

The old man nodded. "I was still in there when I heard somebody running down the drive. I looked out the window in time to see a man in uniform running away, and I figured it must be the soldier. The papers were full of his wife's death, and it seemed likely he might be worried about the letter, too. That's the reason I hung around La Rene's Place Saturday night—just in case he came back to his old hangout and I could give him the letter and ease his mind. Sure enough, he did, but he was drunk and didn't recognize me. Just got mad. The next day I burned the letter with the trash."

The old man finished his recitation and looked around helplessly for some verification. Wilma nodded from the divan, but nobody noticed her now.

"Very thoughtful!" Curtis snapped. "I don't suppose it ever occurred to you that a hero could also be a wife killer!"

"That's a lie!" Blade screamed. "I didn't kill Jeri! I didn't even set foot on this place until after I heard she was dead! Sure, I was scared about the letter, but it didn't mean anything!"

For a man who had been tongue-tied so long, Blade could do all right once he got started. Osgood let him get everything off his chest—the threatening letter, the fool things he'd written in the shock and pain of learning that the woman he loved was throwing him over. It must be rough at that, Osgood thought. Rough enough to make a man kill—if he was that kind of a man.

And then suddenly everything was quiet again, because Blade had run out of words and everybody in the room was looking at the man who claimed to know the answer.

Osgood sighed. "So that was the way things stood the day Phillip Blade came looking for his wife," he said. "An interesting addition to my man hunt, but not so interesting when his alibi checked and Ruby Lennox was found murdered. Of all possible suspects, Blade had the least reason to kill Ruby unless her death was a cold-blooded attempt to implicate Wilma Rathjen. It wasn't, of course. It was a very deliberate attempt to eliminate her. I realized that this afternoon when I tried to turn on the lights in her apartment."

Wilma sat bolt upright. "The lights went out," she announced. "All the lights went out at once, and Ruby went to fix them."

"Yes, Miss Rathjen, all the lights went out because the switch was pulled. And Ruby never came back from her mission because it's easy to make a mistake in the darkness. It must have been quite a shock to the killer to realize that the wrong woman had been silenced; but then it began to work out even better that way. You ran away and everything was just dandy—because our killer was so afraid of what you *might* have seen that he overlooked what you had."

Osgood still carried the torn photograph in his pocket. He took out the pieces and fitted them together on the top of Ann Jenner's coffee table.

"The one link that could lead to a murderer," he said. "One more question, Miss Jenner. You told me yesterday that the bath water was running when you returned to Jeri's apartment with those sleeping pills. Did you turn off that water before you left?"

Ann's startled eyes were answer enough. "Why, no. But someone must have turned it off."

"Yes, someone. Someone who was in that apartment all the time, because it wasn't a telephone conversation that you overheard in the bedroom, and all those pointed remarks Jeri made weren't just for your benefit."

Osgood paused to read the frightened faces. Only one was important now.

"An old admirer had just presented her with this picture," he continued, "an old admirer who would dig up anything out of a past he knew only too well in order to stop a marriage that would deal him out for good. Oh, he must have known about Phillip Blade. He'd known Jeri since her modeling days and that was long before she picked up an allotment at La Rene's bar. But Blade was temporary. Blade was just an insurance risk. However, when Jeri announced her intention of marrying Doctor Fergus, she also announced her death. Isn't that right, Tony?"

There was a kind of collective gasping sound in the room from which only Tony Carmen refrained. Maybe he'd been expecting this all along. Maybe that's why he'd run so far down that alley before he remembered that alleys can have dead ends.

"I don't know what you're talking about," he choked. "Jeri wasn't my girl!"

"You weren't listening, Tony. That's just what I said."

"But you think I killed her—"

"I know you killed her, Tony. I would have known a lot sooner if Miss Rathjen hadn't made such a co-operative suspect; but then, maybe it's just as well that she did run away from Ruby's body. It loosened a lot of tongues—including yours. You were the one who put me on the right track to Jeri's unidentified date; but I knew Fergus wasn't the killer as soon as I found this photograph and traced it to her apartment."

Tony didn't seem to appreciate photography any more, and Osgood didn't blame him. Between a neglected art collection and a neglected light switch, he had a right to look unhappy.

"Once I found this photograph," Osgood continued, "all I had to do was identify the one in this tight-lipped group who knew Jeri Lynn's photographer. Someone, for instance, like a trumpet player who once tried to do an act with her at La Rene's Place."

Even then Tony must have known he was finished; but he wasn't used to wearing ropes.

"You're crazy!" he yelled. "You've just got it in for me!"

"The way you had it in for Miss Rathjen when you started the fire tonight?"

"I started the fire?"

"You were at the ladder."

"Because I was after the guy! I ran after the guy for a couple of blocks!"

Nobody argued with Tony. He was yelling all by himself when the front door opened and Frenchy walked in. "I just talked to headquarters," he said. "Poole broke down and is singing like a canary."

"Poole—"

One word and Tony knew the final score. Osgood let him add it up for himself. Hunter Poole, a man with a camera for hire and a file of lens studies only an old acquaintance could know about. Going to Poole for that photo made it natural to call on him for a scouting detail; and fearing Wilma Rathjen made it natural to steer suspicion her way. But it hadn't worked. In spite of everything, she came home again, and a woman sane enough to be freed was sane enough to testify—if she lived. Frightened people shouldn't murder, Osgood thought. They try too hard.

"Poole has a bruise on his jaw that just about matches the skinned knuckles you showed me Saturday night," he said dryly. "You needn't have been so worried about his free-lancing. Curtis Rathjen doesn't believe in reporting attempted blackmail."

"I was thinking of my sister," Curtis protested.

"That's the trouble with this case. Too many people

have been thinking about too many other people—all except Tony. Tony never thought about anything but himself and the girl nobody else was going to have if he couldn't. What was the matter, Tony, were you double-crossed? Were you the one originally slated for Fergus's spot when Blade came home and Jeri got her annulment?"

Tony looked like a man standing at the edge of a precipice. The closing odds were all posted, and there was nothing to play but a long shot.

"All right, shut up about it!" he cried. "Sure, I killed Jeri but it was an accident. I was in the bedroom, like you said. After the nurse left, I went into the living-room to try to talk some sense into the girl, but she was out cold. I didn't know what had happened. I took her into the tub to revive her and that fool hair dryer fell in the water."

"With the switch on," Osgood reminded.

"Okay, so I hit it with my elbow!"

"The same elbow that hit Ruby Lennox?"

Tony didn't speak another word.

By this time the fire was out and the firemen were dragging their hoses over poor old Wallace Timm's broken and battered hedges. The excitement could die down now and the crowds drift away just as they had after Jeri's body was removed. Phillip Blade could go back to camp and try to forget he ever had a wife; Curtis Rathjen could go home and call a psychiatrist for himself; Denise and Sharl could put greater depths into their next portrayal of tragedy; and Dr. Fergus could try to understand why a nurse he took for granted stuck her neck out so far just because she'd taken his threat too literally. As for Wilma, she seemed quite content now that everything had been explained. Evil uncovered never bothered her.

It was time to fill out one of those reports again, but at the door Osgood stopped and turned around. "There's just one more thing," he said, while all of those people came to attention. "I'm still puzzled about that birthday cake. Somebody must have had a birthday last Wednesday. Who was it?"

"Last Wednesday?" Ann repeated slowly. "Why, that was Donnie's birthday. Jeri must have ordered the cake for Doctor Fergus's little boy."

There was a choking sound from the divan, and everybody looked at Wilma.

"Donnie!" she gasped. "That's it! I knew all along that I made some mistake on that order. The inscription wasn't supposed to be 'Happy Birthday Darling,'—it was 'Happy Birthday *Donnie*'!"

And then she sighed and leaned back against the cushions, smiling. "I'm so glad Mrs. Waggoner never found out," she said. "It would have caused such a lot of trouble."

The End

Helen Nielsen was born in
Roseville, Illinois, on October
23, 1918, and studied
journalism, art and
aeronautical drafting at
various schools, including the
Chicago Art Institute. Before
her writing career, she worked
as a draftsman during World
War II and contributed to the

designs of various aircraft. She wrote 18 novels and
nearly 50 short stories—mostly for *Alfred Hitchcock's
Mystery Magazine*—also writing scripts for such
television dramas as *Perry Mason* and *Alfred Hitchcock
Presents*. Her stories were often set in Laguna Beach and
Oceanside, California where she lived for 60 years
before retiring in Arizona, passing away in Prescott on
June 22, 2002.

Black Gat Books

Black Gat Books is a new line of mass market paperbacks introduced in 2015 by Stark House Press. New titles appear every three months, featuring the best in crime fiction reprints. Each book is sized to 4.25" x 7", just like they used to be. Collect them all!

Haven for the Damned
by Harry Whittington
978-1-933586-75-5 $9.99

Only the Wicked
by Gary Phillips
978-1-933586-93-9 $9.99

Eddie's World
by Charlie Stella
978-1-933586-76-2 $9.99

Felony Tank
by Malcolm Braly
978-1-933586-91-5 $9.99

Stranger at Home
by Leigh Brackett writing
as George Sanders
978-1-933586-78-6 $9.99

The Girl on the Bestseller
List by Vin Packer
978-1-933586-98-4 $9.99

She Got What She Wanted
by Orrie Hitt
978-1-944520-04-5 $9.99

The Persian Cat
by John Flagg
978-1933586-90-8 $9.99

The Woman on the Roof
by Helen Nielsen
978-1-944520-13-7 $9.99

Stark House Press

1315 H Street, Eureka, CA 95501 707-498-3135
griffinskye3@sbcglobal.net www.starkhousepress.com

Available from your local bookstore or direct from the publisher.